HOW I SURVIVED MIDDLE SCHOOL

It's All Downhill From Here

Check out these other books in the
How I Survived Middle School series by Nancy Krulik

HOW I SURVIVED MIDDLE SCHOOL

It's All Downhill From Here

By Nancy Krulik

SCHOLASTIC INC.

New York   Toronto   London   Auckland   Sydney
Mexico City   New Delhi   Hong Kong   Buenos Aires

For Suzanne, whose phone calls keep me sane!

ISBN-13: 978-0-545-05259-7
ISBN-10: 0-545-05259-9

12 11 10 9 8 7 6 5 4 3 2   9 10 11 12 13 14/0

Printed in the U.S.A.
First printing, January 2009
Book design by Steve Scott

When Push Comes to Shove . . .

Taking a stand isn't always easy. But for some people, it's nearly impossible. What about you? Are you as sturdy as a boulder when it comes to speaking up for your rights? Or do you have a few footsteps on your forehead from people walking all over you? Are you a pushover or not? To find out, take this quiz!

1. **You've been practicing your hook shots and free throws all year in the hopes of making the basketball team. And it paid off, because you did pretty well in tryouts. But when the team is posted on the gym wall, your name isn't on the list. What's your immediate reaction?**

    A. Walk away. Maybe basketball's just not your sport after all.

    B. Storm into the coach's office and let him know what an unfair jerk you think he is!

    C. Calmly knock on the coach's door, explain how hard you've worked, and ask him to reconsider his decision.

2. **Your mom has had a rough day at work. By the time she gets home, she's grumbling and cranky. She starts growling at you for leaving the living room such a mess. That particularly stings, since it was your brother who made the mess. What's your response to Mom's outburst?**

A. Growl back and tell her you've had just as lousy a day as she has, and you refuse to clean a mess your little brother made.

B. Let her grumble a little. She obviously needs to vent.

C. Wait until she chills a bit, then tell her you're sorry she had such a rough day and explain that she's treated you unfairly.

3. **Your aunt has volunteered to take you shopping for a dress for the school dance. She's picked out a ruffled red-and-white checked dress, but you have your eye on a sophisticated black number. What do you do?**

A. Sweetly explain that while her choice is cute, you'd really feel prettier in the black one.

B. Tell her that if you can't have the dress you want, you don't want anything.

C. Take the red-and-white ruffled dress home with you. After all, your aunt's being generous, and it's really not *that* bad.

4. **Your former BFF tells everyone at school that you still sleep with your old baby blankie. That's *très* embarrassing! How do you deal?**

A. Ignore everyone's laughing and pointing. It will all blow over in a day.

B. Announce her worst secret — *she still sucks her thumb* — over the school PA system. That'll show her!

C. Call her at home and ask her to cut it out. After all, you know plenty of secrets about her, too.

5. Your grandma is visiting for your birthday. When your friends come over to help you celebrate, she keeps calling you "Sugar Bear" (her pet name for you) in front of them. What do you do now?

A. Grin and bear it. Your pals will understand. After all, they have grandparents, too.

B. Keep your mouth shut about the embarrassment during the party. Later you can explain to your grandma that you're getting too big for that nickname.

C. Tell her to stop it right then and there! You're not a baby anymore, and it's time for her to give up calling you by such a childish name.

6. Your Spanish teacher surprises your class with a pop quiz. The boy next to you tries copying from your paper, and the teacher spots it and gives you both zeroes. What do you do?

A. Wait until class ends, then go up to the teacher and explain that you honestly had no idea he was copying and you don't feel you deserve to be penalized for his actions.

B. Start shouting immediately about how unfair the teacher is, and then threaten to get your dad, the *lawyer*, involved.

C. Take your zero, and then study really hard so you can make it up by getting a better grade on the next quiz.

7. **Your best friend borrowed your favorite jacket, and returned it with a huge hot chocolate stain. To make matters worse, now she wants to borrow your new boots. What do you do?**

A. Tell her you'll loan her your boots — as soon as she cleans your jacket.

B. Refuse to loan that slob anything ever again!

C. Loan her the boots. A little stain is nothing to risk a friendship over.

8. **Yay! It's a hot and sunny Saturday. You're psyched to hit the beach! But your pals want to be the first ones to see the new sci-fi thriller at the cineplex. Where are you headed?**

A. To the movies. You'd rather not make a big stink about it. Besides, you had planned to see the movie eventually.

B. Suggest a compromise — how about the beach in the morning, and the movie in the late afternoon?

C. Head off to the beach by yourself — who needs friends around when you've got the sun and surf, anyway?

Now it's time to total up your score.

1. A. 1 point   B. 3 points   C. 2 points
2. A. 3 points   B. 1 point   C. 2 points
3. A. 2 points   B. 3 points   C. 1 point
4. A. 1 point   B. 3 points   C. 2 points
5. A. 1 point   B. 2 points   C. 3 points
6. A. 2 points   B. 3 points   C. 1 point
7. A. 2 points   B. 3 points   C. 1 point
8. A. 1 point   B. 2 points   C. 3 points

What Does It All Mean?

8–12 points: It's nice to be nice, but you've taken politeness to an extreme! You let people force you to go against what you really want. Start standing up for yourself. People won't hate you for it — they'll actually respect you.

13–19 points: You know how to stand up for yourself. The great thing is you also understand that yours is not the only point of view. What you have is a rare gift — the ability to stand up for yourself without hurting anyone's feelings. Bravo!

20–24 points: No one will ever accuse you of being a pushover! In fact, you refuse to bend . . . ever! Unfortunately, insisting on always having your own way will eventually leave you mighty lonely. You need to learn which battles are important enough to fight, and which ones you can let slide.

Chapter

ONE

SPLASH!

I leaped back just as a big, green truck drove through a puddle of slush by the side of the road. Unfortunately, I didn't jump fast or far enough. In an instant, my jeans and shoes were covered with a cold, wet mix of snow and mud. Yuck!

Just then I heard some giggling coming from the other side of the school bus stop. I looked over and saw Addie Wilson laughing hysterically into her cell phone. "You should have seen what just happened, Maya," she said. "Jenny McAfee just got covered with slush! It's okay, though. It's not like she ruined a nice outfit or anything."

My face turned beet red. Addie was always making nasty comments about the clothes my friends and I wore. But she was wrong. I knew my pants were cool. They were skinny red jeans, just like the ones in the teen magazines my friend Chloe has strewn around her room. There was no snow on the ground, so I'd figured it would be safe to wear them with my regular shoes. Of course, I hadn't considered the slush still left by the curb.

Actually, more than being upset by what Addie had said, I was kind of amazed. She was only standing a few feet away from me, yet somehow, Addie had managed to avoid being splashed by the truck. Her jeans and shoes were completely slush-free. I wasn't surprised, though. Being covered in slush just wasn't something that happened to Addie — or to any of the Pops, for that matter.

The Pops. That's what my friends and I call Addie and her group of friends. They're the popular kids in our school. You know — the ones who always have the best clothes, makeup, cell phones, and stuff. Every school has a group of Pops. Sometimes they're called the Queen Bees or the Cool Kids. But whatever you call them, they all have one thing in common. They're a very exclusive group that just about everyone wants to belong to.

I realized I didn't have a chance at being a Pop on my very first day of middle school. Even though Addie and I had once been best friends, she made it clear the minute I ran into her in the hallway that our friendship was finished. Over the summer Addie had dumped me. No explanations, no apologies. When I left for sleepaway camp we were friends, and when I came back we weren't. Just like that. And now she was a Pop, and I wasn't.

Brrr . . . A cold, icy wind started to blow. My legs went numb under my wet, red jeans. I crossed my legs and rubbed them together for warmth.

"Ha! Now she looks like she has to go to the bathroom," Addie told Maya. "No, I swear. She's doing the pee-pee dance like a little kid. She may as well go in her pants. They're already soaking wet." She started to laugh again.

As I listened to Addie giggling into her cell phone I frowned and made a face at her. I wanted her to know I'd heard what she'd said, and I thought it was pretty mean. Of course, she took just that moment to use her phone to take my picture. *Grrr* . . . Now Addie was sending a photo of my goofy face to all of her friends. Any second now they'd all be laughing at me. I don't know why that bothered me so much, but it really did!

I got on the bus and grabbed a seat near the front. Addie took her usual seat in the middle of the bus. Addie was the only Pop on our bus, so she sat alone. She would never share a seat with a non-Pop. She'd rather walk!

I, on the other hand, always shared a seat with my friend Felicia, who got on at the stop right after mine. I started to laugh as soon as she came on board. Obviously, a fast-moving truck had splashed Felicia, too, because her jeans were all wet. And she'd made the mistake of wearing canvas sneakers. Her toes had to be freezing!

"It's not that I mind being cold and wet," Felicia told me as she plopped down in the seat beside me. "But if I'm going to be this way, it would have been nice to have been doing something fun, like sledding or skating."

I nodded in agreement and then sat back in the seat, trying really hard not to think about just how cold, wet, and utterly yucky I was feeling at the moment. Or about how gross school buses smell on wet days.

As the bus turned into the school parking lot, I was surprised by how quiet it was. Usually the parking lot was filled with kids hanging out until the first bell. But today it was just too cold and windy to be outside.

"We can dry off near the radiators before we go to our lockers," Felicia suggested as we walked inside.

"Sounds good," I agreed.

Unfortunately, everyone seemed to have had the same great idea. All the radiators in the cafeteria were surrounded by kids trying to warm up and dry off before starting their day. Since our bus was one of the last to arrive, Felicia and I were going to have to drip dry.

Our friend Rachel was sitting on a chair at the far end of the cafeteria. We hurried over to hang out with her for a few minutes before the bell rang. "I see you guys got splashed, too," Rachel said, pointing to her damp pant leg. "Considering it hasn't snowed in three days, there sure is a lot of slush out there."

"I know," Felicia agreed. "My feet are freezing."

A playful smile formed on Rachel's lips. *Uh-oh,* I thought to myself, knowing what was coming. That was Rachel's joke-telling smile. No one in school told more jokes than Rachel. Or worse ones, for that matter.

"You know how to keep your feet from getting frostbite, don't you?" Rachel said.

"How?" Felicia asked, falling right into her trap.

"Don't go outside *brrrrr*foot!" Rachel giggled.

Felicia and I rolled our eyes.

"Did you guys hear the one. . ." Rachel said. But before she could get the words out, the bell rang.

"Saved by the bell," Felicia teased.

"Come on," I urged my friends. "We've got to get to our lockers. This morning's already started out terribly. I don't want to be late for English, too."

BE A BUDDY!!!

As I walked into my first period English class, I stared at the words that my teacher, Ms. Jaffe, had written across the chalkboard. Ms. Jaffe wasn't in the room at the moment, but she had obviously wanted us to notice what she had written.

"What's that about?" I asked my friends Sam and Chloe as I sat down in the seat beside them.

Chloe shrugged. "I don't have a clue," she said. "But it must be important. She used three exclamation points."

Sam nodded in agreement. "Ms. Jaffe is keen on using punctuation, isn't she?"

I grinned. I always love when Sam uses expressions like "keen on" in her British accent. Did you ever notice that whenever people from England speak, they always sound so much cooler than the rest of us?

In fact, Sam *is* cooler than the rest of us. Today she had a red streak in her hair (left over from our recent Spirit Week), and she was wearing black leggings with black-and-white striped shorts over them. If I'd worn that, I'd look ridiculous. But Sam was cool enough to pull it off.

Even the Pops thought so. I could tell by the way Addie and her friend Dana Harrison were looking at Sam.

"I can just hear Ms. Jaffe." Chloe laughed. She pushed back her shoulders and raised her neck up like Ms. Jaffe. "I have *such* exciting news for you," she said in a perfect imitation of our teacher's high-pitched voice.

"Chloe, that was aces," Sam said between giggles. "You sounded just like her."

I nodded in agreement. I wasn't sure what *aces* meant, but I could tell it was a compliment. And Chloe deserved it. She really did dead-on imitations of our teachers.

Just then, Ms. Jaffe walked into the room. Sam and I stopped laughing immediately. Chloe slumped down in her seat and got quiet.

"Good morning, class," Ms. Jaffe greeted us. "I have *such* exciting news for you."

Chloe, Sam, and I all started to giggle. We couldn't help it. She sounded just like Chloe had predicted.

"Is something funny, girls?" Ms. Jaffe asked us.

Everyone turned and stared at us. I could feel my face turning beet red. No surprise there. I blush all the time. It doesn't take very much to get me started.

"Um . . . no, Ms. Jaffe," Sam said as she choked back her giggles. "It was nothing you said or anything."

Ms. Jaffe gave her a strange look, and shook her head. "Okay, if you have all the laughing out of your systems, I will tell you the wonderful news. Joyce Kilmer Middle

School is starting its very first buddy mentoring program. Isn't that terrific?"

We all just stared at her. We had no idea what a buddy mentoring program was.

Ms. Jaffe sat down behind her desk. "Let me explain," she said. "A mentor is someone who gives advice and support to someone who is younger and less experienced. Students who sign up for this program will spend one afternoon a week at Lincoln Elementary School doing fun projects with kindergartners. The older children will be buddies for the younger ones."

Dana immediately raised her hand.

"Yes, Dana?" Ms. Jaffe asked.

"Does that mean if we sign up to be a buddy we get out of our afternoon classes one day a week?" she asked.

"Uh-oh," Chloe murmured from her seat behind me. But she didn't sound too upset, since it was Dana who was about to get in trouble.

"She totally just dropped a clanger," Sam agreed in a whisper only Chloe and I could hear.

I figured "dropped a clanger" meant made a mistake. In which case, Sam was absolutely right.

"This is not about missing classes," Ms. Jaffe told Dana sternly. "This is about wanting to help younger students. It's about doing something for the community."

Dana looked shocked, like she couldn't believe anyone — not even a teacher — would speak so firmly to her. She was a Pop, after all.

But I wasn't one bit surprised. Pop or not, Dana had just broken one of those unwritten rules that you never find in the official middle school handbook. I was keeping a running list of them in my head.

MIDDLE SCHOOL RULE #29:

NEVER TELL A TEACHER THAT YOU'RE VOLUNTEERING FOR SOMETHING JUST TO GET OUT OF CLASS OR HOMEWORK. TEACHERS WANT YOU TO VOLUNTEER FOR NON-SELFISH REASONS.

I was definitely going to volunteer for the buddy mentoring project — and not just because I could get out of some classes. I actually like being around little kids. I'm an only child, so I don't have any younger brothers or sisters to hang around with. Also, I'm thinking about being a kindergarten teacher when I grow up. The buddy mentoring program would be a good way for me to see if I really like it. But I still had a few questions for Ms. Jaffe, so I raised my hand.

"Yes, Jenny?"

"Who comes up with the projects that we do?" I asked my teacher. "I mean, is there a manual or something?"

Ms. Jaffe shook her head. "The older students come up with the ideas, which means you get to be creative. And if you're unsure about whether or not something is appropriate for kindergartners, you can always ask me, or the kindergarten teacher in the room."

I smiled. We could come up with our own fun things to do with the kids! This was sounding more and more exciting by the minute.

"Now remember, if you sign up to do this, you've made a commitment. You'll be paired with a kindergartner, and he or she will be depending on you to be there every week," Ms. Jaffe told us.

That was fine with me. I'm very reliable. Well, usually, anyway. Sometimes I forget to put the milk back in the refrigerator and stuff like that. But I would never flake out on a little kid.

"I'll have the sign-up sheet on my desk," Ms. Jaffe continued. "If you're interested, stop up here on your way out of class and put your name on the list. In the meantime, take out your books. Let's get started on chapter twelve."

When class ended, I jumped up out of my seat and ran to Ms. Jaffe's desk. I wanted to be the first one to sign up for the buddy program. Sam signed her name right below mine. Then Chloe signed her name, too. We were the only three to sign up, which was fine with me. Chloe and Sam were the two people in my English class that I would most want to spend an afternoon with.

I noticed Dana and Addie standing back, waiting to see who had signed up. I don't know who they were looking for exactly. They were the only two Pops in our English class. I figured if Dana didn't sign up, Addie wouldn't. And if Addie didn't sign up, Dana wouldn't.

A feeling of joy washed over me. Since neither of the Pops in our class were signing up, it was a good bet none of the Pops in the other classes would, either. That would mean I could have an entirely Pop-free activity. Yeah!

Then Ms. Jaffe did the worst thing ever. She complimented us. "Chloe, Samantha, and Jenny, I am so proud of you for signing up. You are really showing how much you care about the community. The children will be able to learn so much from you."

That was all it took. I could see Addie's expression change instantly. First she looked shocked. Then she looked mad. And I knew why. Addie, like most of the Pops, was used to being the center of attention. But today, my friends and I were the ones getting praised by a teacher. And she didn't like that one bit.

She also wasn't about to let it happen. "Come on, Dana," Addie said, pulling her friend by the arm. "We have a lot to teach little kids."

"We do?" Dana asked her.

Addie rolled her eyes. "Of course we do," she insisted. "More than *they* do."

Dana shrugged and followed Addie up to the teacher's desk. I watched as Addie signed her name, dotting her "i" with a little heart just to make it special.

Apparently, I wasn't the only one who noticed. Chloe groaned. "A heart," she murmured. "How goofy."

But I didn't think it was goofy. I thought it was kind of cool. I wished there was an "i" in my name so I could dot it with a heart, too. For a moment I considered changing the spelling of my name to Jenn*ie*, just so I could. But that would be *really* goofy.

Ms. Jaffe studied Dana's face. "Dana, I hope you're not just doing this to get out of going to class," she said.

Dana shook her head. "Oh, no," she assured the teacher. "I really want to do something with little kids."

I definitely wasn't falling for that. But apparently, Ms. Jaffe was. "Well, good for you, Dana. And you, too, Addie. The kindergarten kids will be so lucky to have you. I know you'll teach them a lot."

Addie smiled so brightly I thought her teeth would pop out of her mouth. "Thank you, Ms. Jaffe," she said. "And I'm sure I'll learn a lot from them, too."

Ms. Jaffe looked thrilled. "That's exactly what I'm hoping will happen, Addie. How insightful of you to feel that way."

Addie turned and shot me a smug look. I sighed. Once again, Addie Wilson had stolen the spotlight from my friends and me. Gee, what a shock.

Chapter
TWO

"OH, MAN, not hot dogs again," my friend Carolyn groaned as she stepped up to the counter in the lunch line.

"And broccoli," her twin sister, Marilyn, added with disgust.

"That's just gross," they both added at the same time.

I smiled. "There you go again," I teased.

"It's a twin thing," Marilyn and Carolyn replied at the exact same time, with the exact same shrug.

"You know, I saw this show on TV that said sometimes twins can read each other's minds," I told them.

"It's true," Marilyn said.

"Totally," Carolyn agreed. "Like I know right now Marilyn's wishing she'd brought a bag lunch."

Marilyn nodded. "You're right."

"How did you know that?" I asked Carolyn.

Carolyn held up her hot dog. It was gray and limp. "Who isn't wishing that right now?" she answered.

She had me there. I walked past the hot dogs, and instead placed a bowl of chicken noodle soup, an apple, and a carton of milk on my tray. Then I followed the twins over to the table where my friends and I always sit during fifth period lunch.

Liza, Marc, and Josh were already at the table. Like the twins, Liza and Marc are seventh graders. Josh is a sixth grader, like me. Well, not *exactly* like me. He's actually taking seventh-grade math because he's kind of a genius.

"Where's Chloe?" Marc asked me.

"She's in the lunch line with Sam," I told him. "They'll be here in a minute." I sat down and took a bite of my apple.

"So, did any of your teachers tell you about the new buddy mentoring program?" Liza asked me.

I nodded excitedly. "I was the first one to sign up in my English class," I said. "I think it's going to be so much fun."

"I signed up, too," Liza said. "I like working with little kids. They're so funny."

I nodded. Liza is actually amazing with younger kids. I've seen her around her little brother Spencer. He's in third grade, and he likes to snoop when her friends are over. But no matter how annoying he gets, Liza never yells at him. She just suggests other things he could do that would be more fun. She's really patient.

"I think it would be fun to do art with them," Liza continued. "Like maybe we can have them draw an elephant for the letter E, or a zebra for the letter Z."

"Are you guys talking about the buddy thing?" Chloe asked as she and Sam sat down at our lunch table.

Liza nodded. "Did you sign up?"

"Jenny, Chloe, and I did during English today," Sam said. "How about you guys?"

The twins both shook their heads. "We've got too much going on," Marilyn said.

"With after-school sports and homework and stuff," Carolyn added.

"Same here," Josh said. "Math club meets once a week, and I have to go to tae kwon do right after school at least three times a week if I want to get my second degree black belt."

I understood. Sports did take up a lot of time. "I don't think Felicia or Rachel will be able to sign up, either," I said. "They both signed up for that new athletics club at the community center. That's two days a week."

"I'm not too into working with kids," Marc admitted. "But I said I would tape some of the sessions for the film club."

"Oh, good!" Chloe exclaimed. "I'm thinking about teaching the kids a fifty states song. You could film us doing that." She began to sing. "Alabama, Alaska, Arizona, Arkansas, California, Colorado, Conn—"

"Save it for the kids, mate," Sam teased, playfully putting her hands over her ears. "This jelly is hard enough to swallow as it is." She looked down at the bowl of slimy green Jell-O on her tray.

"I keep telling you it's Jell-O, not jelly," Chloe said. She wasn't the least bit upset about Sam teasing her, though. Chloe's one of those people who can laugh at herself without getting embarrassed.

"This buddy thing's going to be awesome," I said. "I can't wait to start."

"Maybe we should all get together and try to come up with ideas for things we can do with them," Liza suggested.

"Yeah," I agreed excitedly. "I don't have a student council meeting this afternoon, so maybe you guys could come over to my house after school." I stopped for a minute and looked over at Josh, Marc, Marilyn, and Carolyn. I hadn't meant to leave them out just because they hadn't signed up for the buddy program. "I mean, you guys could come, too. We can use all the ideas we can get."

Josh shook his head. "Sorry, but I have tae kwon do right after school today."

"We can't make it, either," Marilyn said.

"Our grandmother's coming over," Carolyn explained.

"Mom wants us home to see her," they finished in unison.

"I can't come over, either," Marc said. "I have to do a live videocast of today's girls' volleyball game. But here's an idea. You can give the kids disposable cameras, have them take pictures, and then write stories about the photos. I loved doing that when I was little."

"Great idea! Thanks!" I exclaimed. Then I turned back

to Samantha, Chloe, and Liza. "Now we only have to come up with about a billion more interesting, fun ideas for little kids to do."

"We'll do it. Especially since we're starting right away," Samantha assured me. "I'll ring my mum during the day and let her know I'm going home with you."

"I'll be there," Chloe said. "I just have to go home and walk Bingo first."

"It must really stink to have to walk a dog in cold weather," Josh said.

Chloe shook her head. "I don't mind. Bingo loves it. You should see him in the snow. He prances like a deer or something. I swear!"

"That sounds so cute," Liza said.

It did sound cute. And for just a single moment, I felt a little jealous of the fact that Chloe had a dog. But that went away really quickly. I have pets too, after all. Two mice – Cody and Sam. They may not prance in the snow (they don't go out of the house – or even out of my room), but they're really cute, and I love them.

"Just make sure we have snacks," Chloe continued, looking down at her food. "This hot dog is too nasty to eat." She pushed her tray away. Then she reached down and pulled something out of her backpack.

"What are you doing?" Marc asked her.

Chloe held up a ball of cranberry-colored wool and two knitting needles. "I'm making a scarf."

"I didn't know you knew . . ." Carolyn began.

". . . how to knit," Marilyn said, finishing her sister's sentence.

"My aunt taught me." Chloe held up her knitting needles to show us the five or six knitted rows she'd already completed.

I looked at Chloe's project. There were a few loose stitches, but for the most part, it looked pretty good. "Nice," I said.

Chloe smiled and sat back in her chair as she began to knit. Her fingers moved slowly, and I could tell she was being really careful. Obviously, knitting wasn't as easy in real life as it looked when grandmothers in the movies sat in rocking chairs and knit little baby booties.

Just then, Addie and Dana and their friends Maya, Sabrina, and Claire all paraded past us. I glanced up at the clock. Lunch was half over. The Pops were right on schedule. They all went to the girls' room together at the exact same time every single day. But it wasn't like their bladders were on the same schedule or anything. The Pops don't actually use the girls' room as a bathroom. They use it as a sort of clubhouse. They go in there to put on makeup and talk about people behind their backs. The Pops do a lot of that.

But today, they didn't go straight to the girls' room. Instead, they stopped by our lunch table.

"Check out Chloe," Sabrina said with a snide tone.

"What are you knitting?" Dana asked.

Before Chloe could even open her mouth to reply, Maya chimed in. "I hope it's a new shirt. The one you have on is awful."

I looked over at Chloe. At the moment she was wearing a yellow long-sleeve T-shirt that read, *I'm So Wonderful, I'm Jealous of Myself!* It wasn't exactly high fashion or anything, but it was totally Chloe.

The Pops all began to laugh. But Chloe didn't say a word. She just sat there, knitting away. And after a few seconds, the Pops moved on. I guess since they didn't get the reaction they'd hoped for, there was no reason for them to stick around anymore.

I smiled at Chloe. I was seriously impressed. If that had been me, I would have been blushing like crazy with embarrassment over what had just happened. I might have even teared up a little bit. But Chloe was cool as could be.

"The Pops are such idiots," she said as she started the next row on her scarf. "They think they know all the cool trends, but they've obviously missed knitting. All the movie stars are doing it these days. It keeps them busy while they're waiting around on the set."

I wasn't the least bit surprised that Chloe knew that. She always knows what the movie stars are doing. She reads tons of celebrity magazines. She says she's doing research so she'll know how to act when *she's* a famous actress.

"Chloe's right," Marc agreed.

Now *that* surprised me. Marc and Chloe are neighbors, and they've been friends forever, but they hardly ever agree on anything.

"Making movies can take a long time," Marc continued. "They have to set up all the lighting and the camera angles and stuff. So actors have to come up with things to do while they wait."

"Exactly," Chloe said with a smile. She looked at me. "Do you think we could teach the kindergartners how to knit?"

"I don't know," I said. "It looks kind of hard. And Liza, Sam, and I don't know how to knit, so I doubt we'd be good teachers. Maybe we could do an easier craft."

"I'm so bummed that Addie and Dana signed up for the buddy program," Sam groaned.

"They did?" Liza didn't sound too happy about that. Not that I blamed her. None of us liked the Pops much.

Sam nodded. "They put their names on the list in English class."

"*After* we did," Chloe pointed out. "This time *we* set the trend."

Liza sighed. "Well, if Dana and Addie signed up, you know the others won't be far behind. They all do the same things."

"One collective brain," Chloe joked.

"Yeah, well, we'll have fun, anyway," I told Liza, Chloe, and Sam. "Starting this afternoon at my house!"

* * *

That afternoon, Chloe, Sam, Liza, and I all got on my school bus together. We took the two front seats on both sides of the aisle — Chloe and Sam shared one seat, and Liza and I shared the other. The minute we sat down, we all started talking about our ideas for what we could do with the kindergartners.

"Even though Felicia can't do the buddy program, she did give me a great idea," I told my friends. "She suggested that we get the kids in a circle and have them toss a ball around to one another. When they catch the ball, they have to say a letter, and something that begins with that letter."

"I get it," Chloe said. She rolled a piece of paper into a ball and tossed it to Sam.

"A – apple." Sam grinned and tossed the ball to me.

"B – baseball," I said as I caught the paper ball. I tossed it to Liza.

"C – cat," Liza added. She popped the ball up in the air and across the aisle toward Chloe. Unfortunately, at just that moment, Addie climbed onto the bus. The wad of paper smacked her in the face.

"Hey!" Addie shot Liza a dirty look. "What'd you do that for?"

"Sorry," Liza apologized.

"You could've hurt someone," Addie said.

"Oh, come on," Chloe groaned. "It's just a piece of paper."

"I could have gotten a paper cut on my cheek," Addie

insisted. But I could tell even she knew she was stretching it. "What were you doing, anyway?"

"It's a game we're thinking about playing with the kindergartners in the buddy program," I told her. "We're spending the afternoon coming up with things to do with them. We want them to have fun while they're learning."

Addie snickered. "Jenny, you always take everything so seriously," she told me. "They're kindergartners. They think *everything* is fun."

"I don't know. . . ." I began.

"Oh, come on," Addie insisted. "How hard will it be to keep a bunch of five-year-olds happy? Read them a story. Give them milk and cookies. You don't need a whole meeting about what to do with them."

I thought about that. Addie was probably right. Still, it couldn't hurt. And my friends and I would certainly have a lot of fun planning things, anyway. We always have fun when we're together, no matter what we're doing. I picked up the paper ball. As Addie walked by, I tossed it over to Sam.

"D – dog!" I shouted out happily.

Chapter
THREE

"THESE ARE SO SCRUMPTIOUS," Sam said as she took a huge bite of a hot s'more. "I don't know who came up with the idea of putting chocolate, marshmallow, and graham crackers together, but they should get an award."

I giggled. Sam was totally addicted to s'mores. In fact, she asked for them every time she came over. Not that I ever complained. I was happy to make them. I love chocolate just as much as she does. I took a huge bite out of my s'more. "*Mmmm* . . . This one is absolutely perfect."

"They all are," Liza told her. "It's pretty hard to mess up a s'more."

"Speaking of messing up," Chloe said. "Did you guys hear what happened to Dana Harrison in math class?"

We all shook our heads.

Chloe sat up taller, obviously pleased that she knew something before everyone else did. "She bombed her math test again. Now she has to go back to being tutored by someone in the math club. I hope it's not Josh."

"Why not Josh?" Sam asked. "He's so good at math."

"Yeah. But he's tutored Dana before. And Felicia was all freaked out about it," Chloe told her. "I mean, he's her boyfriend, but he was spending a lot of time with Dana and . . ."

"She wasn't freaked out," I told Chloe. "She just didn't know what was going on."

Chloe shrugged. "Maybe. But she seemed upset to me. And if Josh has to spend time with Dana again . . ."

I frowned. I don't really like talking about other people. It makes me feel uncomfortable. So I decided this was a good time to change the topic. "If you guys are all finished, maybe we should start making a list of things to do with the kindergartners."

"Good idea," Liza agreed. She gobbled down her last bit of s'more.

"I couldn't eat another bite," Sam said. "Can we work in your room, Jenny? I'd love to see my namesake."

I grinned. Some people might have been upset about sharing their name with a mouse. But Sam, she loved it. In fact, she was crazy about my pet mouse Sam. So much so that whenever she left my house, I always made sure to give Cody lots of extra attention, since my friend Sam usually ignored him.

Sure enough, as soon as we got upstairs, Sam-my-friend took Sam-the-mouse out of his cage and began to pet him. Luckily, Liza picked up Cody and gave him some attention. Chloe pulled out her knitting and began clicking the needles together.

"Okay, so what ideas do we have so far?" I asked, pulling out a pad and pencil.

"Well," Liza began, "we have Marc's idea about the photos, and Felicia's idea about the ball game."

Chloe laughed at the mention of the ball game. "Wasn't Addie ridiculous? A paper cut? Give me a break."

"She did act like a complete nutter," Sam agreed.

"She's also kidding herself if she thinks working with little kids will be easy," Liza said. "My brother's in third grade, and sometimes it's impossible to keep *him* happy and busy. Can you imagine how tough it will be with five-year-olds?"

"People go to college to learn to teach little kids," I added. "So it must be hard to do."

"Can you imagine what would happen if the Pops had a meeting like this?" Chloe asked. "Nothing would get done. They'd just wind up putting on makeup and talking about people. That's all the Pops ever do. I swear, they're such gossips."

Suddenly Sam burst out laughing.

"What's so funny?" Chloe asked her.

"You," Sam told her.

"What?" Chloe demanded.

"You get on the Pops' case for gossiping, but you do plenty of it yourself," Sam explained lightheartedly.

"I do not!" Chloe insisted so loudly that Cody started to squeak in Liza's arms. Liza stroked his back to soothe him and then placed him back in his cage.

"Oh, come on, Chloe," Sam said.

Chloe shook her head. "I don't gossip." She looked at

Liza and me. "Tell her, you guys."

Liza and I looked at each other. We didn't know what to say.

"Well, you were kind of gossiping about Josh and Felicia downstairs," I suggested quietly.

Chloe frowned. "That wasn't gossip. I was just telling Sam what had happened between them. It was before she moved here."

No one said anything. We didn't want to hurt Chloe's feelings any more than we already had. We just wanted to let the whole thing drop.

But Chloe wasn't about to do that. "I'm not a gossip, and I can prove it! Jenny, turn on your computer. There's got to be a quiz on middleschoolsurvival.com about gossiping. I'll take the quiz and prove I'm not a gossip."

"Okay," I said. I sat down and turned on my computer. I didn't doubt Chloe. Middleschoolsurvival.com would definitely have a quiz she could take. It was a pretty incredible website. I'd discovered it at the beginning of the school year when I was looking for some fashion tips for school clothes. It had the tips, as well as recipes, advice, and lots of personality quizzes to take. We all check the website on a regular basis.

"Here's a good one," I said as I scanned the list of quizzes. "It's exactly what you're looking for, Chloe."

Instantly my friends all huddled around the computer so we could read the questions together.

Hey, Did You Hear About . . . ?

Gossip. It's all around us. If you listen hard enough, you can hear the scoop on just about everyone, even if it's not true.

Are you the kind of the girl who grinds the gossip mill, or do you tend to keep your nose out of other people's business? To find out what your gossip grade is, take this quiz. Come on, give it a try. Everyone's talking about it!

"Okay, Chloe," I said. "Here's your first question."

1. Talk about a bummer! Your friend tells you in confidence that she'll be moving at the end of the school year. What do you do with this news?

A. Tell everyone right away. This is too important to keep to yourself!

B. Only tell your closest friends. You have to start planning that bon voyage party ASAP!

C. Keep it to yourself. Your friend will let people know when she's ready.

Chloe studied the question for a minute. I could tell she was taking this really seriously. Finally, she answered, "I guess B. I wouldn't tell everybody, but I think people who really care would want to know in time to plan something."

"B it is," I said as I clicked my mouse over the second response. Instantly the next question appeared.

2. During a phone conversation, your pal lets it slip that she's got a crush on that cute guy in your history class. How do you handle this scoop?

A. Only tell your close group of friends. You know they'll never use it against her.

B. Drop a few hints to the hottie — it's your job as a friend to help them get together.

C. You don't tell a soul, but offer to help your friend if she wants you to.

"It's between A and C," Chloe said. "If one of us had a crush, I know we'd all want to help. But I don't know if I'd want all of my friends to know about it if I was the one with the crush. Wow. This is hard."

"Just say what you'd really do," Liza said. "You have to tell the truth or the quiz won't work."

"Yeah. If you can't be honest with your computer, who can you be honest with?" Sam joked.

"Exactly," Chloe agreed with a smile. "So I'll say C. I wouldn't say anything to anyone."

I clicked the letter C and watched as a new question popped up.

3. There's a surprise party being planned for your best friend! Unfortunately, you know she hates surprises. Now what do you do?

A. Tell the party planners she hates surprises.
B. Warn your pal. Now, at least the party won't be a surprise to her.
C. Say nothing. You're not planning the shindig, so it's not your place to ruin the surprise.

"I would say B," Chloe told us. "I think my loyalty would be to my friend. It wouldn't be my place to ruin the party, since I wouldn't be the one planning it, but I'd at least want my friend to know."

"I know I would appreciate it if someone did that for me," Liza told her with a calm smile. "I hate surprises. I'd rather know so I could be prepared."

"I'll remember that," Chloe assured her.

I clicked on the letter B and watched as the next question appeared on the screen.

4. Do you read gossip magazines?

A. Oh, yeah! The more the better! Celebs want to be gossiped about. That's why they do what they do.
B. Sometimes — like if I'm at the doctor's office.
C. Nah. I'm not particularly interested in other people's lives, no matter how rich or famous they are.

"A!" Liza, Sam, and I all shouted out at once. We didn't need to wait for Chloe to answer at all. We'd all seen the piles of celebrity magazines all over her room.

Chloe giggled. " I do love those things," she agreed.

But the next question that appeared wasn't as easy. In fact, Chloe looked confused as she read it.

5. You just found out your archenemy has been dumped by her boyfriend. This is big news. What are you going to do with it?

A. Tell everyone you know. Finally, she's gotten what she deserves.

B. Tell your closest pals — they know your history, and will share in your triumphant mood.

C. Keep it to yourself. Why lower yourself? She's not worth it.

"It *is* kind of satisfying when someone who has been mean to you gets what she deserves," Chloe mused. "But I don't know if I'd tell the whole school. I don't need to stoop to that level. But I know you guys would want to know. I mean, we all have the same archenemies, right?"

We didn't say anything. None of us wanted to influence Chloe's answer.

"I guess it's B," Chloe said finally. "I would just tell you guys. The rest of the school would find out sooner or later, anyway. It doesn't have to come from me."

As I clicked on the letter B, the quiz ended. We waited as the computer calculated Chloe's answers.

You answered 1 A, 3 B's, and 1 C.

What do your answers say about you?

Mostly A's: You are the queen of the gossip machine! But beware: Girls who gossip are usually the ones who are most gossiped about!

Mostly B's: You can be trusted, to a point. But sometimes you let info slip. Hey, you're only human. Just try to keep the gossip to a minimum — and make sure you're not doing it to be malicious.

Mostly C's: Your lips are sealed. You can be trusted with anyone's secret, any time!

Chloe stared at the screen, reading what the quiz had said about her. Then she shrugged. "Well, at least I'm not a huge gossip," she said. "It could've been worse."

"True," Liza said.

"Besides, I kind of like knowing what all the movie stars are up to," Sam said.

"I know," Chloe said. "You're almost as into that as I am."

"It's fun reading about it," Sam agreed, "even though I don't think half the stuff in those magazines is really true."

"I think it is true," Chloe said. "Like what they said about that cute kid from that new show about the zoo-keeper's family that's on Monday nights. He . . ."

Uh-oh. I had a feeling this was about to turn into an afternoon of entertainment news from Chloe. And that's not what we were here for. "Come on, you guys," I urged my friends. "We're supposed to be here to plan things to do for the buddy program."

"Oh, yeah, right," Chloe said. "I almost forgot."

"Me, too," Sam admitted.

"Well, we really need to get back to it," I said. "Does anyone have any ideas?"

"Kids like to rhyme," Liza suggested. "Maybe we could have them make up a story using rhyming words."

"That's great!" I added it to our list.

"We should definitely do something active with them," Sam said. "Maybe duck, duck, goose. Do you guys play that here?"

"Oh, yeah," Chloe told her. She reached over and patted Sam on her head. "Goose!" she shouted.

Sam immediately leaped up and began chasing Chloe around the room. Chloe hopped up on my bed and leaped over the pillows toward the closet.

Before Sam could tag Chloe, though, my mom appeared at my door. "Hey, girls, it's starting to snow," she told us. "How about I drive you all home before it really begins to come down?"

"Do you think we'll have a snow day tomorrow?" Chloe asked excitedly.

"I don't know," my mom told her. "But anything's possible in the winter."

Chapter
FOUR

WHEN I GOT UP THE NEXT MORNING, there was a light layer of white snow on the ground. But it wasn't enough to cause a snow day, unfortunately. So I crawled out of bed and began to get dressed. I made sure to tuck my jeans into my warmest waterproof boots. Then I put on my down coat and a hat and gloves so I could stay as warm and dry as possible as I trekked to the bus stop.

Apparently, most of the kids in school had the same idea. When our bus pulled up, I saw a lot of kids hanging out in the parking lot. Everyone was wearing boots, ski coats, and warm gloves and hats. They were the perfect outfits for a massive snowball fight — which was exactly what was happening!

Splat! A snowball hit my back the minute I stepped off the bus. I turned and saw Marc grinning at me.

"Man, you were an easy target!" he exclaimed.

"Yeah, that's 'cause you hit me in the back. But now I'm ready for you," I warned as I bent down and picked up a nice big blob of fresh snow. "You're doomed!"

And with that, Marc took off across the parking lot. I followed close behind. A moment later, Marilyn and Carolyn were beside me, snowballs in hand.

"Marc got us, too," Marilyn explained.

"So we're after him!" Carolyn added excitedly.

"Three against one. We can't lose!" I exclaimed as I ran even faster toward Marc.

But Marc wasn't about to give up without a fight. In fact, he'd enlisted Rachel, Felicia, and Josh to his side. And the snow battle was on.

As I pelted snowballs at my friends, and wiped some of their returned ammunition out of my eyes, I caught a glimpse of Addie. She was standing off to the side with some of the other Pops. Maya and Sabrina were peering into their tiny mirrors and putting on makeup. Dana was braiding her hair. Addie was just watching the snowball fight. I had a feeling she would have wanted to join in — if she could have. But snowball fights weren't a Pop kind of thing. You could get wet and messy during a snowball battle. And Addie would never allow herself to be seen that way in school. Or anywhere else for that matter.

For a moment I felt sorry for my former friend. But that didn't last long. An oncoming slew of snowballs drew my attention away.

"Gotcha!" Rachel shouted.

"Oh, yeah?" I answered back. But before I could throw a snowball back in her direction, the bell rang. The fun was over. It was time to get to class.

"I'll get you all later," I playfully told my friends as I ran inside. "When you least expect it, expect it."

*   *   *

By the time I took my seat in English class, I was cold and wet – again. Pretty much everyone was – except Addie and Dana. They looked perfect. Of course, they hadn't had any fun, either.

Ms. Jaffe walked into the room, looked at her class of wet kids, and started to laugh. It was the first time I'd seen my usually strict teacher really lose it like that. But I didn't blame her. We all looked pretty funny with our wet hair and pants.

"There's something about snow . . ." Ms. Jaffe began. Then she looked at the open textbook on her desk. For a moment I thought she was going to tell us to open to page 74, which was where our homework reading had begun. Instead, she slammed the book shut. "Let's do something different," she said. "Take out a piece of paper."

We all pulled out sheets of paper. "Are we having a pop quiz?" Dana asked nervously. Obviously, she hadn't done the reading the previous night.

Ms. Jaffe smiled. "Nope. We're going to draw snow-flakes." She picked up a piece of chalk and drew a pretty six-pointed snowflake on the board. "Make yours big enough to fill most of the page," she told us with a big smile on her face.

I exchanged glances with Chloe and Sam. *How weird was this?*

"When you finish drawing, I want you to write one snow-related word at each of the points on your snow-flake." Ms. Jaffe said. "It will be a kind of visual poem."

I spent a lot of time drawing my snowflake. It was a while before I began to write my poem. But, eventually, I came up with five good adjectives: wet, frosty, pale, slippery, quiet. But I still had one more to write.

As I was thinking, I glanced over at Chloe's drawing. The picture was nice enough. But the words were strange. She had written: man, ball, day, shoe, fall, and angel.

I couldn't figure out what she was doing. And then it came to me. Those were all the second half of snow words: snowman, snowball, snow day, snowshoe, snowfall, snow angel. I was impressed. That was really clever.

"While you're working, I want to let all of you who signed up for the buddy program know that tomorrow you will be going to Lincoln Elementary School for the last period of the day. It will be your first meeting with your kindergarten buddies, so please don't forget."

Sam raised her hand. "I have a math test last period tomorrow," she told Ms. Jaffe.

"Mr. Kaye will let you take it the next day," Ms. Jaffe assured her.

Sam smiled. "That's great," she whispered to Chloe and me. "I need an extra night to study. This is turning out to be a great day."

I looked up at my suddenly playful English teacher. Then I glanced at my smiling friend, and the pretty snowflake drawing on my desk. There was definitely something special about this morning. As I glanced out the window at the white branches on the tree, the sixth snow word I'd been searching for suddenly came to me. I picked up my pen and wrote it in big letters:

MAGICAL

It was really weird walking into the kindergarten classroom at Lincoln Elementary School the next afternoon. Lincoln hadn't been my elementary school (I went to Washington Elementary), but this classroom could have easily been my kindergarten room. I remembered having a job chart on the wall, with pictures instead of words beside the names. I also remembered the big weather chart with the sun, clouds, raindrops, and snowflakes. Today there were gray clouds and a few snowflakes posted on the chart, since it had been snowing flurries all day long.

The only difference between this room and my old kindergarten room was the size of the chairs and the desks. I remembered them being much bigger in my classroom. These chairs seemed kind of small and low to the floor. Of course, back then I was a lot smaller, too.

Right now, the kindergartners were all sitting in a circle in their meeting area. I realized from the looks on their faces that we must have seemed practically like grown-ups to them. It was a pretty strange feeling.

"Welcome, buddies," Mrs. Cooperman, their teacher, greeted us. "We're so glad you could join us today."

We middle-schoolers just stood there, smiling. We weren't exactly sure what to do or say next.

"How about we match up each pair of buddies, and then you can spend the rest of the time getting to know each other?" Mrs. Cooperman suggested. "Okay, which of you is Jonathan?"

A tall eighth grade boy with glasses raised his hand. "Me," he said in a slightly shy voice.

"Great. Your partner will be Max," Mrs. Cooperman said, pointing to a little kid in gray corduroy pants and a blue sweater. "Why don't you two go over to that corner and get acquainted?" As Jonathan and Max walked off, Mrs. Cooperman continued with her list. "Is Chloe here?" she asked.

"Sure am!" Chloe said, a little too excitedly. The Pops began to giggle. But Chloe didn't even look in their direction. Instead she told Mrs. Cooperman, "I can't wait to meet my buddy."

"I can tell," Mrs. Cooperman said with a grin. "You're paired off with Madison."

I watched as Chloe walked over to the area near the sinks with her little buddy in tow. Madison was pretty cute in her little black-and-white polka-dot tights and denim skirt.

One by one, the rest of us were paired off. My buddy, Sofia, was a cute little girl with big brown eyes and long, curly dark hair that she'd tied up in a ponytail. Sofia had tons of energy. I could tell by the way she jumped up to meet me when Mrs. Cooperman called her name.

Mrs. Cooperman had been careful to match middle-school boys with kindergarten boy buddies and middle-school girls with kindergarten girl buddies. One by one, we paired off and wandered toward different parts of the room.

Since my friends and I had all been planning our activities together, we all gravitated to the same corner of the room, so we could work together as a group. It seemed like it would be more fun for us that way. So Sam and her buddy Carly, Liza and her buddy Shannon, and Sofia and I all went to sit where Chloe had taken Madison. As I plopped down on the floor, I noticed the Pops were doing the same thing. Addie, Dana, and Sabrina were all huddled together in a corner with their buddies – Taylor, Elizabeth, and Jillian. I watched them for a minute, curious to see what they were going to do with their buddies. I had a feeling this wasn't going to be as easy as Addie had predicted it might be.

Still, I didn't watch the Pops for very long. Sofia deserved my full attention. I was *her* buddy, after all. Not that it was hard to give Sofia attention. She was really cute and bouncy. She kept wiggling around, fingering the laces on her pink and green sneakers, and shaking her dark brown ponytail back and forth.

"I love your bow," I told her, pointing to the pink ribbon in her dark, curly hair.

"Thanks," Sofia answered in a high-pitched, little-kid voice. "It matches my sneakers and the hearts on my shirt."

"It sure does," I told her appreciatively.

Sofia nodded. Then she went back to squirming around and playing with her shoelaces. There was a definite lull in our conversation. I figured I should say something else.

"I'm Jenny," I told her. "And I'm in sixth grade."

"Wow." Sofia's brown eyes opened wide. "Are you like a teenager or something?"

I shook my head. "No. I'm only eleven."

Sofia thought about that for a minute. "That's just two away from being thirteen. And thirteen is a teenager."

"You're great at math," I complimented her.

Sofia beamed. "Thanks," she said.

Just then, Chloe took a pile of paper out of her backpack. "Hey, you guys. Let's draw pictures," she said. She glanced around the classroom for a minute "Where does your teacher keep the crayons, Madison?"

"In the art center," Madison told her. She pointed to a section of the room that had art supplies and two easels. "I can get them."

"Great!" Chloe said. "Then we can get started."

A moment later, Madison returned with two big boxes of crayons. "Mrs. Cooperman said to remember to put them back when we're finished," she told us.

"We will," Liza assured her.

"We're a very neat group of mates," Sam added.

Carly, Sam's buddy, began to giggle. "You sound

just like Mary Poppins," she told her. "Can you say *Supercalifragilisticexpialidocious*?"

"Supercalifragilisticexpialidocious," Sam repeated. Carly broke out in a fresh burst of giggles. Sofia, Madison, and Shannon all joined in.

Liza waited for them to stop giggling, and then she explained what we wanted them to do. "Do you guys know how to write your names?" she asked them.

"Of course," her buddy Shannon told her. "We're not babies. You learn how to do that in preschool."

"Oh, I'm sorry. I forgot," Liza said gently. "It's great that you know how to do that because that's how we're going to start getting to know each other. I want each of you to write your names really big in the middle of the paper. And then, I want you to draw pictures of your favorite things all around your names."

"What kinds of favorite things?" Sofia asked.

"Any kind," I told her. "Like your favorite food, sport, or after-school activity. Even your favorite color."

"Oh," Sofia said. "That sounds like fun. I love to draw."

"Me, too," Madison agreed. She picked up a yellow crayon and got started writing her name.

A moment later our buddies were all drawing their pictures. So were Liza, Chloe, Sam, and I. After all, we were buddies, too.

It was fun drawing in a classroom again. You don't exactly get to do stuff like that when you're in middle school. Mostly you just take notes or tests and things like that. That's why I was so excited when Ms. Jaffe had let us draw snowflakes for our poems yesterday. It was kind of rare for things like that to happen.

"Hey, Jenny. Do you like my picture?" Sofia asked. She held up her piece of paper. She'd written her name in big capital letters and she'd drawn a girl holding an animal of some sort. It was hard to tell what animal it was, since it just looked like two circles — one for the head and one for the body. Sofia had drawn eyes and a mouth on the head, and there were four lines coming out of the circle that was supposed to be the body. I guessed those were supposed to be the legs.

I figured Sofia would be insulted if I asked what kind of animal she'd drawn, so I just said. "That's great. Tell me all about it."

"That's me and my cat, Cuddles," Sofia told me.

"Wow, you're lucky to have such a cute cat," I replied.

"I usually feel that way," Sofia told me. She wrinkled her nose. "Except when his litter box needs changing." She pinched her nose.

I laughed. "I know what you mean," I told her. "Sometimes, if I forget to clean the cage my mice live in, it starts to stink."

"You have pet mice?" Sofia asked me.

I nodded. "They're very cute and tiny with soft, white fur."

Sofia thought for a moment. "I don't think our pets could ever be buddies like we are," she told me.

"No," I agreed with a laugh. "I think it would be a good idea to keep my mice as far away from your cat, Cuddles, as possible."

I was having so much fun with Sofia, I didn't even notice the time passing. Before I knew what was happening, Mrs. Cooperman announced, "Okay, boys and girls, time to clean up. Buddy time is over."

"Are you coming back next week, Jenny?" Sofia asked me excitedly.

"Of course."

"Great. I'm going to draw you a big picture of Cuddles, so you can hang it in your room," she told me. "That way, your mice can meet him without getting hurt."

"I think they'd like that," I told her with a grin. "I know I would."

Just then, Elizabeth, Dana Harrison's buddy, came running over to Sofia. "Look what my buddy did to my hair!" Elizabeth exclaimed happily.

Sofia and I both looked at Elizabeth. She had a long French braid going down her back.

"That's so cool," Sofia said.

"It's what the girls are wearing on TV and in magazines," Elizabeth explained to Sofia. "Dana told me so."

I looked over at the Pops' buddies. Elizabeth wasn't

the only one with a new hairstyle. Addie's buddy, Taylor, had her hair twisted into a side ponytail. And Sabrina's buddy, Jillian, was wearing a ballerina-type bun.

"Our buddies took pictures of us with their cell phones," Jillian told Sofia, Shannon, Carly, and Madison. "We pretended we were models."

"What did you guys do?" Taylor asked Shannon.

"We colored pictures," Shannon told her.

"But we do that all the time," Elizabeth said.

"These pictures were different," Madison explained.

"Yeah, we got to draw things we like to do," Sofia added. "And our buddies drew, too. Now we know all about them."

Jillian nodded. "That sounds pretty cool," she said. "Not as cool as new hairstyles, but almost."

"I think it's just as cool," Sofia told her. "I like my hair just the way it is."

Hmmm. This conversation between the Pops' buddies and our buddies seemed oddly familiar. So did the way Taylor, Elizabeth, and Jillian ran off, leaving Sofia, Madison, Carly, and Shannon behind. It felt exactly like what happened all the time at our school between the Pops and my group of friends. But there was no such thing as a kindergartner Pop. Or was there?

Chapter
FIVE

THE NEXT MORNING, there was a thick layer of snow on the ground underneath my window. At least I thought there was. It was hard to see, since there was so much snow coming down outside.

I leaped out of bed and raced downstairs to the kitchen. My mom and dad were already there, drinking coffee and listening to the radio.

"Is it a snow day?" I asked excitedly.

"Not for me," my father said. He folded up his newspaper and stood up. "I've got to get out of here early. I'm taking the bus today. It's going to be slow going."

My dad slipped on his coat and kissed my mother good-bye.

"Bye, Jen," my dad called from the front door.

"Bye," I called back to him.

A moment later, my mom walked back into the kitchen.

"Well?" I asked my mom. "Is it a snow day?"

My mom laughed. "I don't know," she said. "I haven't checked. But you have a computer in your room, you know."

I raced back upstairs to my bedroom and turned on the computer.

There was an excited feeling in the pit of my stomach. I really, really wanted there to be a snow day today. I opened the Joyce Kilmer Middle School website and there it was at the top:

CLOSED DUE TO SNOW.

Woohoo! That was it! I ran back downstairs and danced around the kitchen in my pajamas, screaming with excitement. "YEAH!" I shouted. "Snow day!"

A few minutes later, while I was in the living room, happily watching TV, the phone rang. I knew it couldn't be for me. My friends always call me on my cell phone. It had to be for my mom.

"Hello?" I heard her say. She paused for a minute, listening to the voice on the other end. Then she said, "Oh, hi, Ruth."

I frowned slightly. Ruth was Addie's mother's name. Not that I had anything against Mrs. Wilson or anything. It was just kind of weird that my mom and Addie's mom were still friends, when Addie and I definitely weren't.

"Yeah, the snow's really coming down," my mother said into the phone. She was quiet again, while Addie's mother said something. And then the most horrible thing in the world happened. I heard my mother say, "Of course Addie can spend the day here. I'm sure Jenny would love that. Bring her over whenever you can."

WHAT?

I leaped up from the couch and ran into the kitchen. I must have heard wrong. My mother would never have made plans for me without asking me first. I mean, she hadn't done that since I'd been in the fourth grade. There was no way she would just ruin my snow day like that. Would she?

I came barreling into the kitchen just as my mother was hanging up the phone. She smiled brightly at me. "That was Ruth Wilson. She has to go in to work today. Nurses never have the day off. And just like your dad, she's got to take the bus. No cars can get through this mess, especially on a side street. They haven't been plowed yet."

I looked at my mother strangely. Why was she telling me all this? Wasn't there something a little more important to say right now? Like about Addie? About how my whole snow day could possibly be a complete disaster?

"Anyway, that leaves Addie with no one home," my mother continued. "And she obviously can't be alone all day, so Ruth's walking her over here," my mother continued. "We figured it would be nice for you two to spend the day together."

Nice? *Nice?* How could spending a whole day with my total archenemy be nice? My mother had to know that I wouldn't be happy about this. I mean, I didn't really talk to her about Addie and me not being friends anymore, but she had to have figured it out. I mean, Addie hadn't been over in ages. I didn't even mention her. Was it possible my mother hadn't noticed?

My mother smiled at me. "Now, I know you and Addie haven't been as close as you used to be. . . ." she began.

I frowned slightly. *Talk about an understatement.* Well, at least I knew my mother wasn't totally clueless about Addie and me. But if she knew, why would she tell Mrs. Wilson it was okay for Addie to come over?

"Maybe this will give you two a chance to reconnect," my mother suggested cheerfully.

I sighed heavily. I knew that wasn't happening. I also wondered what Addie was thinking right now. I was pretty sure she didn't want to be coming to my house. So why was she? Why wasn't she hanging out at one of the Pops' houses for the day? That was something I could never ask my mother. She probably didn't know the answer, anyway. I was just going to have to wait until Addie arrived to find out.

About 45 minutes later, Addie and her mother arrived at our house. They were all covered with snow and both their noses were red.

"It's really bad out there," my mother remarked to Mrs. Wilson.

"I know," Mrs. Wilson replied. "But it's supposed to stop in a few hours, so I should be able to pick up Addie by five-thirty or so."

I looked up at the clock on the wall. It was only nine o'clock in the morning. That meant eight and a half straight hours with Addie Wilson. That was not a happy thought.

But Addie seemed fine with it. As she pulled her boots off, she shot my mom a big smile. "Thanks for having me," she said.

"You're welcome," my mother replied. Then, as Addie pulled off her hat, she added, "What a cute haircut. I love your bangs."

I had to admit, my mother was right. Addie's new haircut was really cute. She still had long, blond curls, but now she had bangs, too. The bangs were blown out straight, while the rest of her hair was all curly.

"You didn't have bangs yesterday," I said.

"I decided I wanted them on the way home from the buddy program," Addie explained. "I saw this hairstyle in a magazine and I thought it would look good on me."

"It does," my mother told her. "Doesn't it, Jenny?"

"Um . . . yeah. Sure," I said. "It's a great hairstyle."

My mother smiled. "Why don't you girls go ahead into the kitchen?" she suggested. "I'll be there in a minute and then we can make some special snow day hot chocolate — with lots of mini-marshmallows."

"Yum!" Addie exclaimed. She had a huge smile on her face. "Doesn't that sound amazing, Jen?"

Jen? Addie hadn't called me that all year. It was always Jenny, or actually my full name — Jenny McAfee — when she was making fun of me. But today, it was Jen. Like we were still BFFs or something. Weird.

"Yeah. I love hot chocolate," I said, heading toward the kitchen with Addie. She was actually being kind of okay. Maybe this wouldn't turn out to be such a bad day after all.

But the second we were far enough away so our mothers couldn't hear us, Addie dropped her smile — and her whole friendly act. "I didn't want to come here today, you know," she told me bluntly.

I didn't say anything. I mean, how do you respond to something like that?

"None of my *friends* live in walking distance of my house," Addie explained. "And since my mother won't drive in this snow, your place was my only option."

I rolled my eyes. "It's not like I invited you," I reminded Addie. "My mother didn't give *me* any options, either."

Addie stared at me, surprised that I'd actually answered her back. To tell the truth, I was a little surprised, too. It's really not like me to say something like that. But Addie had made me so mad I couldn't help myself.

Just then Addie's cell phone rang. She pulled it out of her pocket. "Hey, Maya," she said. "No, I can't. I'm stuck at Jenny McAfee's all day."

I sighed. She wasn't the only one who was stuck.

"I'll survive. . . ." Addie said dramatically. "Thank goodness for cell phones. At least I can *talk* to you guys. Just make sure everyone calls me . . . a lot." She was quiet for a minute, listening to whatever Maya was telling her. Then she said, "I wish I could show you my new hair today.

But it will have to wait until tomorrow. I just hope it still looks the same."

I sighed heavily. *Oh, give me a break,* I thought. Of course it would look the same. It wasn't like her bangs were going to grow out overnight or anything.

A moment later, my mom walked into the kitchen. Addie quickly said good-bye to Maya and put her phone back in her pocket. "That was Maya," she told my mother sweetly. "Jenny and I go to school with her. She's in seventh grade."

"Maya," my mother repeated the name. "I haven't heard you mention her, Jenny."

I shrugged. "We're not that close," I said. "She's more of Addie's friend."

My mother didn't say anything. Instead, she got out the cocoa and marshmallows. I got the milk from the refrigerator. As she and I busied ourselves making the hot cocoa, Addie went over to the cabinet and pulled down the mugs.

The smell of chocolate in the kitchen made me a little happier. It's hard to be upset or angry when your whole house smells like Willy Wonka's chocolate factory.

My mom placed two mugs of cocoa on the table. "You girls enjoy," she said. "I've got a load of laundry to put in. See you in a bit."

I frowned. I really didn't want my mom to leave me alone with Addie. I wasn't in the mood to be made fun of this early in the morning.

Surprisingly, Addie didn't make fun of me. She just sipped her hot cocoa. "*Mmmm . . .* this is delicious," she cooed.

"It really is," I agreed, taking a big swig from my mug.

As I looked up, Addie began to giggle. "Um . . . Jenny . . ." she began.

"What?" I asked. I got a little tense. *Here it comes . . .* I thought.

"You have a marshmallow stuck to your nose," Addie told me.

I reached up and felt the tip of my nose. Sure enough, there was a wet squishy marshmallow there. Addie started laughing again. So did I. It was actually pretty funny.

"Yeah, well you have a chocolate mustache," I told her, laughing.

Addie giggled, and licked her upper lip. "Yum!" she exclaimed. "At least it's not scratchy like my *dad's* mustache."

I smiled. For just that moment, it seemed like old times again. Unfortunately, the moment didn't last long. Addie's cell phone rang again, and when she picked it up, she was right back in Pop world.

"No, I can't," she mumbled into the phone. "I have to stay here all day." She paused for a moment, frowned, and then said, "Oh, that sounds like fun. I wish I could, but with the snow this bad, I'm trapped here."

I sighed. Trapped. That was the perfect word. For both of us.

Chapter
SIX

AFTER WE HAD OUR COCOA, my mother suggested Addie and I go hang out in my room for a while. It wasn't exactly the kind of snow day I'd had in mind, but I didn't tell my mother that. There was no point. Obviously, she wanted Addie and I to have things back the way they used to be so badly that she was determined to keep us together all day.

Actually, I understood how she felt. Things certainly were easier back in elementary school. There were no groups of friends. We were all friends together. My guess is that was because we had to be. We all spent the whole day in the same room with the same kids doing the same things. But now that we were in middle school, with different kids in each class, we'd started to break apart and find friends we had things in common with. Addie and I just didn't have that much in common anymore.

Which pretty much explains why Addie switched on her cell phone to talk to her friends the minute we got into my room. I, on the other hand, started to play with my mice. I guess I could have called my friends, too, but they hadn't called me yet, and I thought they might have gone back to bed. Besides, I really didn't like talking on the phone in front of other people all that much, especially in front of someone like Addie. She didn't have to know my private business. Not that she would find it all that interesting, anyway. The Pops never thought anything anyone had to say was particularly interesting unless one of them was saying it.

As I listened to Addie drone on and on about how her new bangs made her look just like some model she and Sabrina had seen in a magazine (Addie had no problem allowing other people to hear her business), I noticed that she wasn't letting the person on the other end get a word in.

That got me thinking. Maybe Addie and I had had a parting of the ways at just the right time. Back when we were in middle school, our friendship had been pretty even. She and I shared everything, even the spotlight. Like when there was a talent show in fourth grade, and Addie and I had written a skit to perform, we'd made sure that we both had the same exact number of lines in the skit so that we were both the stars. But the new Pop Addie wasn't like that. She didn't want to share the spotlight. Not even with other Pops. She was their leader. That was pretty impressive since, like me, she was a sixth grader, and some of the other Pops like Claire and Maya were seventh graders. And Sabrina was an eighth grader!

"Oh, it's easy for me to keep them straight," I heard Addie say into the phone. "I just use my hot iron in the morning, and they stay that way all day long."

I rolled my eyes. Addie's conversation was really dull.

So was petting my mice. They're cute and all, but you can't really talk to them. (Well, actually, I talk to them all the time, but I would never do it when someone else was around. Especially not Addie! The last thing I needed was Addie Wilson thinking that I was crazy.) So I put Cody and Sam back in their cage and turned on my computer. I immediately clicked on my favorite website, middleschoolsurvival .com. I scrolled up and down the screen looking for something interesting. Finally, I found a quiz that seemed perfect, considering what I'd just been thinking about.

Are You Standing in the Shadows?

When it comes to your place in your group of friends, where do you stand? Does your shadow loom large over everyone else, keeping your friends completely out of the spotlight? Or are you one of those people who prefers resting in the shade to dancing in the sun? If you want to know whether or not your friends are overshadowing you, answer these quiz questions.

1. **Click! The yearbook photographer has just taken a snapshot of you and your pals hanging around outside the school. Where can you be found in the photo?**

   A. In the center of the group — telling a story.
   B. Right next to your BFF, who is obviously telling a joke.
   C. A little off to the side, but still part of the gang.

   This was a tough one. I'm not a person who always needs to be the center of attention, but I don't stand off to the side, either. And I don't actually have a best friend. None of my friends really does. We're all BFFs. Still, I'm usually around when Rachel tells a joke. Since that answer was the closest to my life, I clicked the letter B.

2. It's time for club sign-ups! Which activity are you most likely to join?

A. The tennis team. It gives you the best of both worlds. You're on a team, but you still get to play one-on-one competitions.

B. Cheerleading — you love being the leader of a crowd.

C. Nature photography — then it'll be just you and the flowers in the park.

I thought back to when we had club sign-ups in school in the beginning of the year. I hadn't had any idea what to sign up for — until my friends convinced me to go out for student government, and run for class president. I won that election, by the way, by beating Addie Wilson! She's our vice president now. Anyway, since we don't have any cheerleaders in our school, I guess being in student government is the best way to become a leader. So I clicked the letter B again.

3. It's Saturday night! All your homework's done, and you're ready for a totally fun night. What's your plan of action?

A. Stay in and read a good book in a warm bubble bath. Mmm . . . the perfect evening!
B. Go to the movies with your BFF.
C. Drag your whole crowd to the ice-skating rink for a night out.

That one was easy. Ice skating! My friends and I had just done that a week ago. We went to this cool outdoor rink in the park and skated for hours. We were all pretty horrible, and we fell a lot (especially Josh for some reason), but we had a really good time. Letter C it was!

4. Woohoo! It's the school Winter Festival Party. Where can you be found?

A. In the middle of the dance floor trying out some new moves you saw in a video on MTV.
B. At home. You don't really like crowds.
C. With a few of your close buds by the snack table. You're not looking to meet any new people.

I studied the question for a minute, trying to figure out exactly which answer to give. I knew I could cross B out right away, because I go to every school party or dance. I sort of have to, being on student council and all. But I would go anyway. I love my school, my friends, and parties. Why would I stay home? So now it was between A and C. It could be either. Sometimes Chloe drags us all onto the dance floor with her. Chloe is never shy, and when I'm around her, I don't feel shy at all. But I also like to hang out with my pals by the food. Our school usually has some pretty good treats at parties. But as for the part about not wanting to make any new friends, that didn't sound like me at all. I love meeting new people. If I'd closed myself off to new friends I never would have become close with Sam, who started at our school in the middle of the year. My friends and I welcomed her into our group, and we're all really glad we did.

That settled it. My answer was A.

5. You've got a new science teacher. She's trying hard to learn all the kids' names. How's she doing with yours?

A. She keeps confusing you with your lab partner.

B. Yours was the first name she got right all week long.

C. Every now and then the teacher gives you a look of surprise — like she's forgotten you were in her class at all.

I thought back to the beginning of the school year. It did take some of my teachers a while to learn who I was, although I wasn't the only one. And it wasn't like they forgot my face or anything. It just takes people a while to learn a lot of names. So based on that experience, I chose the letter A.

A moment later a new image appeared on the screen:

It's time to total your score.

1. A. 3 points B. 2 points C. 1 point
2. A. 2 points B. 3 points C. 1 point
3. A. 1 point B. 2 points C. 3 points
4. A. 3 points B. 1 point C. 2 points
5. A. 2 points B. 3 points C. 1 point

You have scored 13 points.

What does your score say about you?

5-8 points: You've definitely been hiding in the shadows. In fact, you've been spending a lot of time far from the center of the school social scene. It's not a bad thing to prefer to be on your own. In fact, it's nice that you enjoy your own company. But once in a while, wouldn't it be fun to come out of the shade? You may have to force yourself, but you might find it fun to join in with your group of pals and hit some school events or parties. Give it a try — what do you have to lose?

9-12 points: Congratulations. You've found a nice middle ground. While you don't have an overwhelming need to be center stage every day, you're still where the action is. You're content with who you are. You don't need the whole world to applaud your every move, but you're not so timid that you won't venture out into the spotlight when you need to.

13-15 points: Overshadowed? You? Never! In fact, it's your shadow that looms large over your friends. You're always the center of attention. While that can be fun for you, it may also grow tiresome to the people who are around you. Why not take a moment to stand back and give your pals a chance to shine once in a while? They'll appreciate it for sure!

Well, that was interesting. I'd never thought of myself as a center-of-attention kind of person. But I guess other people could view me that way, especially because of the whole class president thing. I also had a feeling that if any of my friends had taken that quiz they would have gotten a similar answer. We kind of take turns being the center of attention.

Just then, I heard my cell phone ring. Yeah! Finally one of my friends was calling. I was happy to hear from them, of course. But I was also happy that Addie would see that she wasn't the only one with pals who wanted to spend the snow day with her.

I checked the caller ID. "Hi, Marc," I answered. "What's up?"

"What are you doing?" he asked me.

I glanced over at Addie and sighed. "You wouldn't believe me if I told you," I replied.

"Try me."

"Well, I'm sitting in my room watching Addie Wilson talk on her cell phone," I told him. "Her mom had to go to work, and my mother volunteered to have her hang around here all day."

"Oh," Marc said. "Well, maybe your snow day can still be spared."

"How?" I asked.

"Now that the snow is stopping, Chloe, the twins, and I are heading up to Fender's Hill to go sledding," Marc told me. "Why don't you and Addie meet us there?"

I frowned. Fender's Hill was very steep. My mom had never let me go sledding there before. "Let me call you back," I said. "I have to ask my mom first. She's always been kind of freaked out about how steep Fender's Hill is."

"Okay," Marc said. "We're going to leave in about half an hour."

"I'll go ask her now," I promised. Then I hung up my phone and started to head downstairs.

"Where are you going?" Addie asked as she hung up her phone.

"Marc just called and asked me if I wanted to go sledding on Fender's Hill," I told her. "I'm asking permission."

"Fender's Hill?" Addie asked. "Your mom will never go for that."

I frowned. Addie was probably right. She knew my mom almost as well as I did. But I wasn't giving up without at least trying. "I'm going to ask, anyway," I told Addie.

"She'll say no," Addie insisted as she followed me downstairs.

We found my mother in the family room, folding some laundry. She looked up and smiled as we walked in. Great. She seemed like she was in a pretty good mood.

"Hey, Mom. Marc just called and asked if I . . ." I stopped and pointed to Addie. "I mean, if *we* could go sledding with some kids on Fender's Hill." I knew including Addie in the request would definitely please my mother.

"Fender's Hill?" my mother asked. "Jen, you know I don't like that steep hill."

"But that doesn't make any sense. When we go skiing, you let me go on the intermediate slope. That's way steeper than Fender's Hill," I pointed out.

"But that's at a ski resort. There are adults all over, not to mention safety patrols and ski instructors. You can get help if you need it," my mother reminded me.

"Mom, there will be a zillion kids — with cell phones — at Fender's Hill. We can call for help if we need to," I told her. "We're not little kids anymore. We're in middle school. And we're more responsible."

My mom considered that for moment. "Well, I guess, if you check in every now and then, and let me know you're okay. . . ." she began.

"Oh, we will," I said excitedly. "Right, Addie?"

Addie sighed. "I don't want to go sledding," she told my mom and me. "I don't like steep hills. They scare me."

I stared at Addie. Was she really doing this to me? It had to be a joke. . . . Or not. The look on Addie's face was serious.

"Oh," my mother said. "Well, that settles it, then. Jenny, Addie is your guest. You have to take her feelings into consideration."

I thought about reminding my mother that I hadn't been the one to invite Addie over, but I knew that wouldn't help. "Fine," I said angrily. "Whatever *Addie* wants." I knew I didn't sound very gracious, but it was still a lot nicer than what I'd *wanted* to say.

I trudged out of the room with Addie behind me. She didn't even apologize for totally ruining my day. I guess that was because she wasn't sorry for doing it. Frankly, I didn't believe her whole being-afraid-of-steep-hills speech. I think she was actually afraid of showing up at Fender's Hill with a non-Pop. Being seen with me might damage her reputation.

When I got upstairs, I called Marc back. "I can't go," I told him.

"Your mom said no, huh?"

"No. My *mom* was about to say yes. Then *Addie* said no," I explained. "Apparently she doesn't like steep hills. And she's a guest, so . . ."

"Oh. I'm sorry, Jenny," he said sincerely.

"Me, too," I replied. "I guess I'll see you tomorrow, if we have school."

"Yeah," he answered. "Hang in there."

"I'll try." As I hung up the phone, I turned back toward my computer. I may have had to stay inside with Addie, but I didn't have to talk to her. I could take another quiz instead.

But Addie wasn't going to let me do that. "I can't believe you told him that," she barked at me.

"Told him what?" I asked her.

"That I'm afraid of steep hills. You knew it was supposed to stay a secret," Addie insisted.

"You never said it was a secret," I replied.

"I thought you'd figure it out. I mean, it's kind of embarrassing," she told me.

I didn't know why Addie was making such a big deal about it. It didn't seem like anything to be embarrassed about to me, but I didn't say that. I knew it had just been an excuse to avoid going out in public with me. I really wished Addie wasn't there.

But Addie kept talking, making it kind of hard to ignore her. "So what can we do?" she asked me. "How about makeovers?"

I sighed. "I don't have any makeup," I told her. "I'm not allowed to wear it yet." Actually Addie wasn't allowed to, either. She kept her lip gloss and eye shadow in her locker. She put her makeup on when she got to school and then washed it off before she left the building. That way her mother never saw her in it.

"I love changing my look," Addie continued. "These

new bangs make me seem completely different, don't you think?"

"They're nice," I said. Actually, that was a lie. Her bangs were a lot more than nice. They were gorgeous. But I wasn't going to tell Addie that.

"It was so easy," she told me. "They took only ten minutes."

Now I couldn't pretend to be disinterested. "Really?" I asked her.

Addie nodded. "It was hard with my curls, but once my hair was wet they were pretty straight and it was a breeze."

Just then, Addie's phone rang again. She glanced down at the caller ID. "Oooh, it's Claire," she said, obviously happy to have one of her Pop pals to talk to. "I have to take this."

"Whatever," I said.

"Hey, Claire," Addie said. "I'm so glad you called. There is absolutely nothing to do at Jenny McAfee's house. I'm bored to tears."

Grrrr. That made me furious. Nothing to do? We would have had plenty to do, if Addie hadn't said she wouldn't go sledding. Addie had ruined my chance to have fun with my friends and now she was trashing me to hers. That was it. My mother could make me stay in the house with Addie, but she couldn't make me stay in the same room with her. I stormed out of my bedroom, slamming the door behind me. Addie wasn't stupid. She had to have known how angry I was. And I was glad.

As I walked down the hall, I passed by the bathroom. I wandered in and looked at myself in the mirror. It was funny. Addie and I were still the same two months apart we'd always been. But she looked so much older and more sophisticated. Especially since she'd cut those bangs.

I took hold of a few pieces of hair in the front of my head. Then I folded them under to make them look like bangs. Wow! I looked really different, and kind of cute. Maybe even *sophisticated.* Just like Addie.

Hmm. My hair was already straight. The bangs would be easy to cut. And Addie's bangs sure did look great. I knew they would look great on me, too. Maybe even better than they did on Addie, since I wouldn't have to straighten them every morning.

And if Addie could cut her bangs all by herself, I knew I could. It certainly didn't seem very difficult. I hurried downstairs and took the scissors out of the drawer in the kitchen. Then I zoomed back upstairs to the bathroom and got to work.

About five minutes later, I knew I was in trouble. I looked in the mirror, studying my reflection. My freshly cut bangs didn't look anything like Addie's. Hers fell along the side of her face in a gentle feathery sweep. Mine were all choppy and uneven. They were a total disaster. Tears began streaming down my face.

"Mom!" I cried out as I raced downstairs.

"What is it?" my mother shouted as she hurried to meet me at the bottom of the stairs. Then she looked at my hair. "Oh, Jenny. What have you done?"

"I wanted bangs like Addie's," I blubbered through my tears. "And she said they were easy to cut, so I figured I could do it."

By now, Addie was on the stairs behind me. "Jenny, why did you cut them yourself?"

"Why not?" I asked her. "You did."

"No, I didn't. My mom's hairdresser did it," Addie told me.

I stared at her in disbelief. She was lying right to my face. "But you said it was hard to cut them curly, so you wet them until they were straight. And then it took you just ten minutes."

"That is what happened. But the *hairdresser* wet my hair, and *she* cut them. I just sat in the chair," Addie said with a smile. "I would never cut my own hair. It might turn out like . . . well, like that." She pointed to my choppy bangs.

I sighed. Now that I thought about it, Addie had never actually *said* she'd cut her own hair. But she'd led me to believe she had. And that was almost as bad. Not that any of that mattered now. "I can't go to school like this," I sobbed. "We have to go to the hairdresser and get them fixed. Now."

My mother sighed. "Not with the snow all over the road," she told me.

"Then what can I do?" I asked frantically.

"Let me see if I can fix them," my mother suggested. "I used to cut your hair when you were little. I can probably do this, too."

A few minutes later, as I sat in my mother's bathroom watching her trim my bangs, I thought about how awful Addie had become. She'd tricked me into this! But then, I thought about it for a minute. I really had no one to blame for this mess but myself. After all, I was the one who had broken a very important unwritten middle school rule.

MIDDLE SCHOOL RULE #30:

FIND YOUR OWN STYLE AND STICK TO IT. DON'T TRY TO COPY ANYONE ELSE. REMEMBER TO ALWAYS STAY TRUE TO YOURSELF.

"There. I'm finished," my mother said a few minutes later. She moved aside and let me take a look in the mirror.

I almost started crying again when I saw my reflection. My bangs were not long and sweeping like Addie's. They formed a straight line right across the middle of my forehead. "They're really short," I whispered.

"I had to cut them that way," my mother explained. "They were so uneven. But they'll grow in."

"They don't look bad at all," Addie told me. I knew she was lying. I could tell by the way her eyebrows were kind of arched up. Her eyebrows always did that when she lied.

"Here, let me take a picture," Addie said. And before I could protest, she'd snapped a shot of me on her camera phone.

I frowned. I knew what she was up to. With the push of a button, Addie had sent my short-banged, tear-stained image through cyberspace to her friends' phones. Any minute now, Pops all over town would be laughing at me.

Not that that was anything new.

Chapter
SEVEN

BY THE NEXT DAY, the roads were clear and the snow had stopped. According to the Joyce Kilmer Middle School website, school was open. I'm sure all of my friends were really disappointed. But they weren't as disappointed as I was. I was hoping I would have another few days for my bangs to at least start to grow in before I had to face the entire Joyce Kilmer Middle School population. Okay, I know that was unrealistic — bangs take more than a few days to grow in — but I was still hoping.

Anyway, I had to go to school. But that didn't mean I had to unveil my horrible hair — at least not right away. I was determined to put that nightmare off as long as I possibly could. So while I tucked my coat, scarf, and gloves away in my locker, I left my hat on. I figured if anyone asked, I could just say I was still a little cold.

I slipped into my English class, and took a seat a little farther from the front than I usually would have. Then I opened up my book and started reading, hoping no one would notice me.

Wishful thinking. The minute Addie and Dana entered the classroom, they began laughing. "Nice hat," Dana said sarcastically.

"Why are you wearing a hat in class?" Addie added between giggles.

"I'm cold," I muttered.

"Must be the lack of hair on your head," Dana told me. She started laughing all over again.

Chloe and Sam walked into the room while Dana and Addie were laughing at me. "What's that about?" Chloe asked.

"Who knows?" I lied. "I never understand what they think is funny."

"It doesn't take much to get them laughing," Sam agreed. "They're so incredibly daft."

"Wow, I love your scarf," I told Chloe, changing the subject as quickly as I could.

"Thanks," Chloe replied. "I finished it yesterday. And I'm glad I did. It's so cold in here, I couldn't bear to take it off."

I grinned. I knew it wasn't cold in the school building. Chloe was wearing the scarf so we could all see it. Not that I blamed her. It was really pretty. Besides, who was I to say anything? I was planning on using the same excuse for keeping my hat on all day.

Just then, Ms. Jaffe walked into the classroom. She went straight to the board and began writing. But before she could get two letters out, Dana called to her, "Ms. Jaffe, I think I remember there being a rule about wearing hats in school."

Uh-oh.

Ms. Jaffe turned around. "You know there is, Dana. No student is supposed to wear a hat or a cap in the school building unless it's Spirit Week."

"Well, Jenny McAfee is wearing her hat," Dana told her.

Grrr. So much for not being noticed. Thanks a lot, Dana.

Ms. Jaffe turned her attention to me. "Jenny, please take your hat off," she said.

"But I'm cold," I replied feebly, knowing perfectly well that wasn't going to work.

"You'll warm up in a minute," Ms. Jaffe assured me. "You know the rule as well as I do."

I sighed. I knew the rules better than most. I was probably the only kid in the whole sixth grade who'd read the middle school orientation handbook from cover to cover. And I remembered the rule about students not wearing hats. They were considered too distracting.

There was no getting out of it. Slowly, I pulled the wool cap off of my head. Almost immediately, Dana and Addie broke into a fresh round of giggles.

I began to blush, hard. Not that that's so unusual for me. I tend to get embarrassed pretty easily. And this time I knew Dana and Addie had good reason to laugh. My new bangs were pretty awful. And I also figured that since I'd been wearing a wool hat, I probably had a combination of hat hair and static electricity. I didn't need a mirror to figure out I looked like a mess.

Sam and Chloe looked at me curiously, but neither of them said a word. And in a minute, all the attention on me was focused elsewhere. Ms. Jaffe turned to Dana. "Since you have such a good memory today, Dana, why don't you tell us what you remember from chapter four of *The Red Pony*?"

Dana gulped. "But yesterday was a snow day. We didn't have school."

"I know," Ms. Jaffe said. "But I assigned this the day *before* yesterday."

"But we all knew there was going to be a snow day, yesterday," Dana told her. "There was going to be a big storm. We heard it on the news."

Ms. Jaffe didn't answer her. Instead, she pointed to someone else. "Chuck," she said. "Can you summarize the chapter?"

As Chuck began to talk, I hid my head behind my book, and tried to remain really quiet and out of sight. I'd already gotten enough attention for one morning.

"What's with the new 'do?" Chloe asked me as she, Sam, and I walked out into the hall together after class.

I sighed. "Addie tricked me into doing it," I said, which wasn't exactly true, but I didn't feel like going into the whole thing again. "I totally hate it."

"It's not so bad," Sam assured me.

I gave her a look.

Sam sighed. "Well, anyway, it's just hair. I change mine all the time."

That was true. Today she had a green streak going down the right side of her head.

"It'll grow in," Sam continued. "And when it does, it'll be really cute."

"And until then, I'll help you come up with a way to camouflage it," Chloe promised me.

"How are you going to do that?" I asked her.

Chloe gave me a smile. "You'll see at lunch," she assured me.

That really piqued my interest. In fact, it was pretty much all I thought about all morning. So I was sort of disappointed when I walked into the cafeteria at lunchtime and all I saw was Chloe sitting and quietly knitting. When I sat down at the table she looked up at me and smiled. "Hi, Jen," was all she said.

I thought about asking her about her big camouflage plan, but then I stopped myself. It's kind of uncomfortable to bug someone when they volunteered to help you. I was just going to have to sit down and talk about something else for a while.

But that was pretty tough to do. Especially since the twins noticed my hair right away.

"Jenny, you got bangs," Marilyn said.

"When did you do that?" Carolyn asked.

"Yesterday," I told them. "I thought they would look good, but I hate them. They're too short!"

"They're not that bad," Liza assured me. "They're gonna be cute when they get a little longer."

"I didn't even notice," Marc said.

At first I doubted that, but then I realized he was probably telling the truth. Guys never notice things like hairstyles or new clothes. I glanced over at Chloe, hoping she would mention her big solution to my problem, but she was still sitting there, uncharacteristically quiet, knitting something out of multicolored wool.

"So tomorrow's buddy day," Liza reminded Sam, Chloe, and me. "You guys want to get together after school today and come up with things to do with the kindergartners?"

"I can't," I told her. "I have a student council meeting. We're planning the winter fund-raiser."

"Any idea what you might do?" Sam asked.

I shook my head. "This is the first time we're talking about it. I'm hoping other people have thoughts about it. This is my first year here, so I don't really know the kinds of things the school's done before."

"Last year we had an ice-skating party," Marilyn said.

"I heard they did that the year before, too," Carolyn added.

Marc nodded. "It's always been pretty successful, so I guess they keep doing it."

"I'm a terrible skater," Josh said. "My rear end is still sore from the time we all went skating. And that was more than a week ago."

I giggled. Josh had spent more time sitting on the ice than skating. "Well, maybe there's something else we could do," I told him. "We'll see."

Just then, the Pops passed by on their way to the girls' room. I put my head down, hoping they would just keep going. No such luck.

"Addie, that picture you sent around doesn't do that hair justice," Claire said, pointing at my head. Apparently no one had taught her that pointing was rude. Not that it would have mattered. Pretty much everything Claire did was rude.

"Yeah, it's *worse* than it looks in the picture," Maya added.

I could feel my cheeks burning as the Pops laughed and then moved on.

"Don't let them bug you," Sam said, wrapping a friendly arm around my shoulders. "They're just jerks."

I nodded slowly. Sam was right. The Pops *were* jerks. But the Pops were right, too. My bangs were horrible.

"Done!" Chloe announced suddenly as she pulled a pair of scissors out of the bag, and cut off the loose thread at the end of whatever she'd been knitting. "Here you go, Jenny." She handed me a large loop made of knitted yarn.

"What's this?" I asked her, turning the loop around in my hands.

"It's a headband. A nice, thick one," Chloe explained. "You wear it over your bangs. There's no rule against knit headbands, is there?"

"I don't think so." I slipped the multicolored band over my head. "How do I look?" I asked her.

"Awesome," Chloe assured me. "Like in a magazine."

"Really?" I asked.

The twins nodded in unison.

"Fab," Sam said. "Totally."

Marc shrugged. "I thought you looked okay before," he told me.

Josh never even looked up from the math problem he was working on.

"I wish I could see what it looked like." I glanced in the direction of the girls' room.

"You don't need to go in there," Liza said. "I have a mirror." She reached into her bag and pulled out a small hand mirror.

I took the mirror from Liza and looked at my reflection. Wow! The headband completely covered the bangs. All you saw was my long hair flowing behind it. "This is perfect," I squealed. "Thanks, Chloe!"

"You're welcome," she told me.

"You did that really quickly," Sam said.

"It only takes about a half hour," Chloe said. "It's small. And I'm getting to be a fast knitter."

"Do you think you could make me one?" Sam asked her.

Chloe nodded. "Sure. I could make one for all of you if you want."

"That would be amazing," Carolyn said.

"Incredible," Marilyn added.

"No, thanks," Marc told her with a laugh.

"Yeah, I think I'll pass, too," Josh added.

We all began to laugh. Even me. I wasn't upset any more. It's amazing how much a bad hair day – or a good one – can change your mood. And now that I had my new headband, this day had taken a turn for the better.

As I walked into the student council meeting, Addie avoided my eyes completely. She'd seen my new headband in gym class that afternoon, and realized that I wasn't hiding because of a bad haircut. I was just hiding the bangs. Thanks to having supportive friends, I was able to find a way to cope.

A moment later, Sandee Wind, the eighth grade class president, walked into the student council office. She sat across the table from Addie. Addie smiled at her, and ran her fingers through her new bangs. She was obviously hoping Sandee would notice her new look.

But Sandee didn't notice Addie's bangs. Instead Sandee turned to me and said, "Jenny, that's the cutest headband! Where'd you get it?"

"My friend Chloe made it for me," I told her proudly. "She knits."

"Do you think she'd make one for me?" Sandee asked.

"I could ask her," I replied.

"Great, because I'd love something like that for the next time I go skiing," Sandee continued. She paused for a minute. "That gives me a great idea! What about doing a day trip to ski at Hover Mountain for the winter fund-raiser this year? It would be nice to have a change. We've done that ice-skating winter party for years and years."

Addie turned pale. "Skiing? That sounds expensive."

Sandee shook her head. "Hover Mountain has package plans for schools. Bryant High School got a good deal last year. I know because my brother went on that trip."

"Skiing sounds great to me," I told Sandee. Several of the other class representatives murmured agreement.

But not Addie. "The skating party is a tradition!" Addie declared. "We can't just change the tradition."

Sandee shrugged. "Why not?" she asked.

Addie didn't have an answer for that. Instead she said, "What about kids who can't ski?"

"There are lessons," I said. "And Hover Mountain has tubing for non-skiers. I know all about Hover Mountain. My family skis there all the time."

Addie shot me a dirty look. I wasn't sure why she was so determined to go skating. Maybe she had just gotten some fancy skating clothes. Or maybe it was because Addie had only been skiing once, when our two families went together a few years ago. I think she took a lesson, and then went to hang out in the lodge. Whatever the reason, Addie did not want to go skiing. Lucky for me, she was outvoted. Joyce Kilmer Middle School's winter fund-raiser would be a ski trip this year.

As the student council meeting ended and we all walked out into the hallway, Sandee came over to me. "I really do love that headband," she said. "And I'm so glad you wore it today. If you hadn't we might not have come up with the whole skiing idea."

"I'm glad, too," I told Sandee. "I love to ski."

"I've only been a few times," Sandee said. "But I'm getting better. And I think I want to try tubing, too."

"That's a lot of fun," I told her. "My dad and I go tubing at least once every time we go to Hover Mountain. You'd be surprised how fast you can fly downhill in an inner tube!"

"I'll call you tonight so we can get started on the details," Sandee told me.

"Cool," I agreed. My eyes drifted off to my right, where Addie was standing. She was glaring at me angrily. I shot her a smile in return. After all, what did I have to be angry about?

Chapter EIGHT

I WAS STILL WEARING my way-cool knit headband the next afternoon as my friends and I walked into the kindergarten classroom at Lincoln Elementary School. The minute I entered the room I could sense something was different. Instead of sitting in a happy circle, the kids were divided into groups. Carly, Shannon, Sofia, and Madison, the buddies my friends and I had been assigned, were sitting together. Taylor, Elizabeth, and Jillian, the Pops' buddies, were in a cluster as well. The boys were all just kind of hanging out together.

"Jenny!" Sofia jumped up and ran to me. "I am so happy to see you. I made you a picture." She handed me a piece of paper with two people drawn on it. One was taller than the other. Under the taller one, Sofia had written JENNY. Under the smaller one she'd written SOFIA. Next to her was some sort of roundish animal, followed by two smaller animals. I couldn't tell what they were, exactly.

"It's you, me, Cuddles, and your mice," she told me. "Mrs. Cooperman helped me sound out your name."

"You wrote it perfectly," I said. The picture was so cute. I just love the way little kids put bird feet on their drawings of people. "I'm going to put it up on the bulletin board in my room, so the mice can see it, too."

"You promise?" Sofia asked me.

I nodded. Then we walked over to where Sam, Liza, and Chloe were already seated with their buddies.

"So, what have you guys been doing this week?" Chloe asked the kindergarten girls.

"We learned to play hopscotch in the gym at recess," Shannon told her.

"Oh, that's fun!" Liza exclaimed. "I love hopscotch. Do you all play together?"

"Well . . ." Carly's eyes drifted off toward the Pops and their buddies.

"*We* play together," Sofia explained. "But Taylor, Elizabeth, and Jillian don't play with us anymore."

I took a deep breath. So I hadn't been imagining things when I walked into the classroom. There was a definite split in the class.

"Yeah, they play fashion show every day," Madison added. "Their buddies said that was a really cool game to play. I think it's boring."

"I think so, too," Chloe assured her.

"And they keep bragging about the really fun thing they're going to do today," Shannon said.

"What's that?" Sam asked.

"They're making paper dolls," Shannon replied.

Chloe frowned. "That's not so fun. I brought something *really* cool for us to do. We're going to knit."

I shook my head. Somehow the idea of giving a bunch of five-year-olds knitting needles didn't seem too smart to me. "Uh . . . Chloe . . ." I began.

Chloe smiled at me. "Relax, Jenny. We're going to use our fingers, not knitting needles." It was like she had read my thoughts! Chloe pulled out balls of thick, stiff yarn and began passing them around. "I found the directions on middleschoolsurvival.com," she told Liza, Sam, and I. "It looked pretty easy, and it said five-year-olds should be able to handle it."

I glanced at the printout Chloe had brought with her. It did seem pretty easy.

Fun and Fancy Finger-Knitting

Here's what you need: One ball of yarn (thick yarn works best) and a pair of scissors. No needles required!

HERE'S WHAT YOU DO:

1. Tie the yarn loosely around your left index finger. Leave a tail of yarn hanging down the back of your hand.
2. Weave the yarn behind your middle finger, in front of your ring finger, and behind your pinky finger.
3. Now loop the yarn around your pinky and repeat the back, front, back weaving pattern until you have two strands of yarn across your four fingers.
4. Place your left hand on your thigh, palm up.

5. Starting with your pointer finger, lift the bottom loop over the top loop and drop it behind your hand. Do this for each finger.

6. Now each finger should have one loop of yarn on it.

7. Once again, weave the yarn in the back, front, back pattern on your fingers.

8. Repeat steps 4 and 5.

9. Keep knitting until you've made a length of wool that is long enough for a headband.

10. Now it is time to finish off. When each finger has only one loop, start from the pinky. Lift the loop off the pinky, and put it on the next finger. There should be two loops on your ring finger.

11. Lift the bottom loop over the top loop.

12. Now lift the remaining loop off of your ring finger and move it to the next finger.

13. Lift the bottom loop over the top loop.

14. Repeat until there is only one loop left on your index finger.

15. Cut the yarn from the ball so that it leaves a six-inch tail.

16. Poke the tail through the loop on your index finger and pull the tail through to make a knot.

It took the kindergartners a few tries, but before long they were all finger-knitting. However, that was more than I could say for myself. Chloe had to show me about ten times before I had it down, but once I did, it came pretty easily. And after a few rows, I could see that what I was knitting was going to be just the right width to be another headband. All I would have to do when I was finished knitting was ask my mom to help me sew the band into a circle.

Our buddies were really having a good time knitting. They were so proud to be making something all by themselves. Even Sofia, who was so wiggly, was sitting still and concentrating on what she was doing. But I had a feeling that finger-knitting wasn't really enough to keep a five-year-old's attention for the rest of the afternoon. I didn't want our buddies to get all bored and antsy. Then I remembered Liza's idea about doing activities with rhyming words.

"Have you guys ever done rhyme time?" I asked them.

"What's that?" Sofia asked.

"We go around in a circle and try to come up with as many rhyming words as we can," I told her.

"Is there a winner?" Shannon wondered.

I shook my head. "Nope. This game's just for fun. There's no competing. And we can do it while we knit." I started the game. "Knit, bit."

"Sit," Sofia said excitedly.

"Kit," Liza added.

As we went around the circle, Sofia smiled up at me. "I like this game, Jenny. Especially because there's no winning or losing. I don't like competing."

I noticed Sofia's eyes drifting over to where Addie and

her friends were sitting with their buddies. "I know exactly what you mean," I told her.

I wasn't happy about the way the kindergarten class was being affected by the conflict between the Pops and my group of friends, but I didn't have a lot of time to think about it. The minute I got home my phone rang. It was Sandee Wind. And, boy, did she have a lot for me to do for the ski trip, starting with making posters.

The next morning I arrived at the bus stop with my two huge posters advertising the trip. The minute Addie spotted me with them, she frowned.

"Are those for the ski trip?" she asked me.

I nodded.

"I don't know why you insisted on that as a fund-raiser," Addie continued. "It's going to stink."

That made me really mad. "I didn't insist on anything," I told Addie. "Everyone voted for it except you. And it's going to be great. You're not always right about everything, Addie Wilson!"

Addie's face turned pink, and her eyes narrowed to tiny slits. "I'm right a lot more often than you are, Jenny. At least I didn't chop my bangs up so I have to wear a headband every day."

"I like my headband!" I insisted. "Everyone does. Sandee told me on the phone last night that she was going to wear one today. She bought it at the mall."

Addie looked shocked. "Sandee called you last night?"

I nodded coolly. "Twice."

Addie wasn't sure what to say about that. And I knew why. It wasn't just that Sandee was an eighth grader. Although, that would have been a pretty big deal. It was also that Sandee was president of the eighth grade class. That made her really important. And the fact that I'd made it clear we hadn't just been talking about student council plans — that we'd been talking about normal friend stuff — obviously surprised Addie.

To tell you the truth, it had surprised me, too. Sandee had never talked to me about anything except school events before last night. But somehow, my headband had shown her that I could be stylish. So now I was cool enough for her to talk to, at least once in a while.

"So I guess you're not going on the ski trip," I said to Addie.

Addie rolled her eyes. "Of course I'm going," she told me. "I have to. I'm on the student council, too. I'm sure Sandee has a job for me to do. Something much more glamorous than just making posters."

"Oh, I'm not just making posters," I told her. "I'm also selling tickets at the volleyball game after school."

"You are?" Addie sounded surprised.

I nodded. "With the seventh grade reps."

"Oh," Addie said quietly. "I wonder why no one asked me to sell tickets. I'm great at sales."

That was true. If Addie gave her Pop stamp of approval to an event, we'd sell tons of tickets.

"Sandee probably didn't think you would want to be involved," I told Addie. "You pretty much dissed the whole ski trip idea at the meeting."

"I didn't dis it," Addie insisted. "I just gave a different suggestion. I never said anything was wrong with having a ski trip."

Now it was my turn to roll my eyes. Addie had a habit of rewriting history so that she looked better. But there was no reason for me to point that out. Besides, I knew she would be a real help selling tickets.

"Well, you could meet us at the volleyball game and help," I told Addie.

Addie cocked her head for a minute, thinking. "Well, if you really need me," she said slowly.

I didn't really need her help. But I didn't say that.

"I bet I could sell more tickets than both seventh-grade representatives combined," Addie said.

"It's not a competition," I reminded her.

"Sure it is, Jenny," Addie corrected me. "*Everything* is a competition."

I sighed. I guess that was true – if you were a Pop. After all, Pops usually came out on top.

Which Addie did, again. By the end of the next day's volleyball game, Addie had sold 50 tickets to the ski trip – more than anyone else. Everyone was impressed, especially Sandee.

"Wow, Addie!" she exclaimed. "Thanks to you, we sold a lot of tickets. That means a lot of fund-raising money for the school. We may even be able to get those two new computers for the library."

Addie smiled. "You know me. Anything for Joyce Kilmer Middle School."

Sandee nodded in agreement. Then she smiled in my direction. "It was smart of you to recruit Addie to help out with sales."

"Thanks," I said, just to be polite. I didn't really feel very thankful about Sandee's comment. It would have been nicer to have been complimented on the 23 tickets I had sold. It wasn't as much as Addie's 50 tickets, but it was still a lot.

"I'm getting really excited about the trip now," Addie told Sandee. "So many cool people are coming!"

Sandee nodded in agreement. "You want to go get a hot dog and a soda to celebrate?" she asked Addie.

"Sure." As Addie walked off with Sandee, she shot me a triumphant glance. Once again her Pop power had triumphed over a mere mortal — me.

Chapter
NINE

I DON'T KNOW if it was Addie's sales prowess, or my posters, or just the idea that a ski trip on a Saturday would be fun, but we had enough kids to fill four buses on the morning of the trip. We also had five teachers who had volunteered to be chaperones for the day.

"Wow, Jenny. You sure have a lot of tags on your jacket," Rachel said as she and I waited to get on the bus with Chloe, Marc, and Liza in the parking lot.

I fiddled proudly with the lift tickets on my ski jacket. "I wore this jacket last winter, too. So most of these are from last year's ski trips." I held one up. "This one's from the trip my family took to Colorado last winter. And this one's from Vermont. Oh, and this one's from Hover Mountain. I was just there last month."

"This is only my third time skiing," Chloe said. "So I signed up for the lessons."

"That's a good idea," I told her. "A lot of kids are taking them."

"I've never skied before," Marc told me. "I figure it's a good time to learn, though."

"It is," I agreed. "And once you get started, you're never going to want to stop."

Liza giggled. "You're like a walking ad for ski resorts."

"Speaking of ski resorts . . ." Rachel began with a grin. "What kind of bird likes to hang around at snowy mountains?"

"What kind?" Liza asked her.

"Ski-gulls!" Rachel replied. She began to laugh at her own joke. "Get it?" she asked.

"Oh, yeah," I assured her. I crossed my fingers, hoping she wouldn't tell us another one.

Luckily, at just that moment, Felicia and Josh came over to us. "Hey, guys," Felicia greeted us. "Ready for the trip?"

"Totally!" I exclaimed. "Are you guys skiing?"

Josh shook his head. "Not me. I'm going to go tubing."

"Me, too," Felicia agreed.

I chuckled to myself. No surprise there. Josh and Felicia usually took advantage of being able to do things together when they could. With their busy schedules, that wasn't always so easy.

"I'm going to try tubing, too," Sam told Felicia and Josh. "I've skied before, but I've never gone down a mountain in an inner tube. It sounds like it would be too much fun to miss."

"The twins are here," Josh announced, pointing to the far end of the parking lot where Marilyn and Carolyn were getting out of their parents' car. They were dressed in identical green-and-blue ski jackets and blue ski pants.

I wasn't even going to attempt to tell them apart. When they got nearer to us I just said, "You two look so great!"

"Thanks, Jen," one of the girls (I'm pretty sure it was Marilyn) said.

"You do, too," the other twin (I think it was Carolyn) added.

"Thanks," I told them. I pulled at the sleeve of my teal green ski jacket. "The jacket's a little old. But I like it too much to get a new one. I always wear this when I ski."

"I think it's cool," Liza assured me. "It's got character."

"Speaking of ski jackets, check out Addie," Chloe said. She glanced over to her left, where Addie, Sabrina, Dana, Maya, and Claire were all standing. Addie was wearing a pink ski jacket with lime green ski pants, lime green gloves, and a fuzzy pink-and-white hat.

"She looks like a professional skier," Liza said.

That was true. Addie *looked* like a professional. But I knew better. I'd been there the only time she'd tried skiing. It hadn't been too successful. But you wouldn't know that by listening to Addie. As we all lined up to board the bus, I heard her talking to her friends.

"There's nothing to it," she was saying. "You just go up on the lift and ski down the hill."

"Aren't you taking lessons?" Maya asked her.

Addie shook her head. "No. It's no big deal. I've skied plenty."

I frowned. Since when was *once* plenty? But I didn't say anything. I didn't want Addie to know I'd been listening to her conversation.

"Don't skiers wear tags on their jackets that show all the times they skied?" Claire asked her.

I smiled and fingered my ski tags proudly. Now Addie was going to have to admit the truth.

Or not. Addie responded to Claire by saying, "This is a new jacket. I thought I'd start fresh on this zipper."

"Oh," Claire answered her. "That makes sense."

Amazing. Addie could talk her way out of anything.

My heart began to pound with joy when the bus pulled into the parking lot at Hover Mountain. I could smell the pine trees, and I could feel the coolness of the air on my cheeks through the bus window. I couldn't wait to get out there and start skiing.

I'll admit that I'm not always the most confident person. I don't like talking in front of people and I get nervous before tests. But when it comes to skiing, I know what I'm doing. That's because I've been skiing since I was a little kid. I practically could ski before I could walk.

Still, I'd promised my mother I wouldn't go on anything steeper than the intermediate trails. I've been on advanced trails before, but only with one of my parents or my aunt, never by myself. Not that I was skiing by myself today, either. Marilyn and Carolyn were pretty good skiers, too. The three of us were planning on skiing together.

"Everyone who has signed up for skiing or snowboarding lessons, please follow me," Mrs. Arlington, a seventh grade science teacher, called out.

Almost immediately, most of my friends headed over to where Mrs. Arlington was standing.

"And those of you who are tubing come with me," Señorita Gonzalez, a Spanish teacher who was also chaperoning, called out.

"That's us," Felicia said to Josh and Sam. She turned to me. "See you later at the lodge, Jenny," she added.

"You bet," I agreed.

"Independent skiers, come with me to rent your skis," Mr. Harding, an eighth grade music teacher, called out. Immediately, I turned and began following him over to the ski rental area. I have my own skis, but it was easier to rent them today than it would've been to bring them. My dad's car has a ski rack, but a school bus doesn't.

Addie, Sabrina, and Maya were right behind Mr. Harding.

"What trail do you want to start on?" I heard Sabrina ask Addie.

"Actually, I thought I would start the day with a hot chocolate," Addie told her. "Let's go to the lodge first, and ski later."

"Are you nuts?" Sabrina asked her. "I only get to ski a few times a year. I want to get as many runs in as I can."

"But I have the cutest sweater on under this jacket," Addie insisted. "I want to show it off."

"You can," Sabrina agreed. "Later."

"But . . ." Addie began.

"Come on," Sabrina insisted. "Let's get skiing before it gets crowded. All you've been talking about is how much you love skiing. Let's do it."

Addie slumped slightly. "Uh . . . sure."

"I think we should start at the beginner slope, though," Maya told her. "This is the first time I've skied all season. I've got to get used to it again."

"Good idea," Sabrina agreed.

Addie shrugged. "If that's what you guys want, it's fine with me."

"Don't look so bummed," Sabrina said. "We can go to a steeper one later."

I didn't hear how Addie answered that one, because the girl at the rental center was handing me my ski equipment. Now that I had my skis in hand, I had much better things to do than listen to Addie, Sabrina, and Maya. It was time for me to hit the slopes!

I spent the morning going up and down a few of the intermediate trails with Marilyn and Carolyn. The twins had been skiing since they were little kids, just like me. We were a good match. Nobody had to slow down for anyone else.

"Hey, Jenny, heads up!" Marilyn shouted as we stood at the top of one of the trails.

As I turned to see what Marilyn wanted, Carolyn hit me in the back with a snowball.

"Gotcha!" Carolyn shouted.

"Tag-team snowball attack," Marilyn joked.

"I'm gonna get you guys," I told the twins.

"You'll have to do it at the bottom of the mountain!" Marilyn exclaimed.

"'Cause here we go!" Carolyn shouted as she and her sister skied off.

"I'm right behind you!" I called to the twins as I followed them down the trail. It was fun being behind the twins, because it gave me a great view of the other skiers watching Marilyn and Carolyn go down the mountain. People on the trail definitely noticed them, probably because it isn't every day that you see two mirror images skiing in the exact same clothes down the exact same mountain at the exact same time. My friends and I are used to Marilyn and Carolyn doing things in tandem. In fact, half the time we don't even notice them finishing each other's sentences anymore. But I could definitely see how strangers would find it interesting.

By the middle of the morning, I was getting hungry. "Hey, do you two want to take a break and go to the lodge for some hot chocolate and maybe a slice of pizza after this run?" I asked the twins as we rode the lift together.

"In a little while," Carolyn said.

"We had a huge breakfast," Marilyn explained.

I'd had a big breakfast, too. But somehow skiing always makes me hungry. And I was practically starving. I was also a little tired. And I know that's when you can get hurt. So instead of going for one more run on an intermediate trail, I decided to take my next run on a beginner trail.

"You guys, I'm going to take one of the beginner trails on my next run," I told Marilyn and Carolyn as we got on the lift for another run. "I'm kind of wiped out."

"Oh," Carolyn said. "Well, we can . . ."

". . . go with you, if you want." Marilyn finished her sister's thought.

"You probably shouldn't ski all by yourself," they said at once.

I looked at the twins. They both had the same disappointed expression on their faces. I could tell they wanted to go for another challenging run on one of the intermediate trails. "It's okay," I assured them. "There are tons of people on the beginner trails. And I'm pretty sure Felicia and Josh will be back at the lodge for lunch soon. Even if they're not, Sam will be. I have a feeling she'll be spending half the day in the lodge drinking hot chocolate."

The twins laughed. We were all very aware of Sam's sweet tooth — especially when it came to chocolate.

"If you're sure," Marilyn said.

"We'll see you in the lodge a little later, then," Carolyn added.

As I skied off the lift and headed to one of the beginner trails, I heard someone crying. I looked around and saw that there was someone hiding behind a big trail map.

Whoever was hiding there sounded so pitiful, I couldn't just ignore it. "Hey, are you all right?" I called out as I skied over.

"Go away," the person answered in a small, scared voice.

I'd heard that voice before, I was sure of it. I peeked around the side of the map, and saw someone in a pink ski coat and a pink-and-white furry hat. "Addie?" I asked, surprised.

"I said go away," Addie sniffled back. But something in her tone made me think she might not really mean it.

"What are you doing up here?" I asked her.

"What do you think I'm doing?" she replied.

"Well, you're not skiing," I pointed out.

"No kidding," Addie said. She sniffled again and wiped her nose with one of her brand-new gloves. Her teeth were chattering. She took one look at me, and the tears really started to flow. "I just can't . . . I really can't," she told me.

"What? Go down the mountain?" I asked. Addie nodded. "But it's just the beginner trail."

Addie shrugged. "It's too steep. You know I don't like steep hills."

I nodded slowly. Suddenly I felt badly that I hadn't believed her that afternoon at my house. I'd thought she didn't want to go to Fender's Hill with me because she didn't want to be seen with a non-Pop. But that hadn't been it. Addie really was afraid of sledding and skiing. "Are you up here all alone?" I asked her.

Addie nodded. "Sabrina and Maya went down a while ago, and that's the last time I saw anyone. They thought I was right behind them, but I've been hiding."

I understood that. After all her bragging, Addie didn't want her friends to know how scared she was. But she had to ski down eventually. "You can't stay up here forever," I pointed out to her.

"I know," Addie replied. "But I'm really scared, Jen."

Wow. That was the most honest Addie had been with me in a long time. Still, it didn't make up for all the mean things she'd said, or the horrible things she'd done to me. No one could blame me if I just left her there and skied down the mountain.

But I couldn't do it. I couldn't just leave her up there all frozen and sad. I mean, I could send someone from the ski resort up to get her, but how embarrassing would that be? Not that Addie didn't deserve to be embarrassed. It's just that I couldn't be the one to do it to her.

"Come on," I said. "I'll help you. We'll go down the mountain together."

Addie looked into my eyes, as though she was trying to figure out if I was seriously going to help her. Then finally, she used her brand-new gloves to wipe her tears away and nodded slowly. "Thanks, Jen," she said quietly as I handed her the ski poles.

"No problem," I assured her.

"Take it slow, okay?" she pleaded.

We did. We skied *really* slowly. Sort of like the way I'd skied the very first time I took lessons, back when I was just a little kid. But I didn't say that to Addie. She was having a hard enough time as it was. I could tell because she wasn't saying a word; she just kept looking straight ahead, trying not to cry. Her face was pale white.

Eventually we got to the bottom. Almost immediately, the color returned to Addie's cheeks, and her breathing got more even. "Thanks, Jen," she told me sincerely. "I don't know how I would've gotten down if . . ."

"Don't mention it," I said. "It was no big deal. And you're down now."

"Yeah," Addie replied with a sigh.

"I'm going to head into the lodge," I told her. "You want to come?"

Addie shook her head. "I think I'm just going to sit here for a minute and catch my breath, you know?"

"Sure," I said. "See you later."

As I headed toward the lodge, I felt pretty good about things. I'd helped Addie, even if she didn't really deserve it. And she'd been really grateful. But I'm not an idiot. It's not like I expected Addie to run and tell her friends that Jenny McAfee was this great person who helped her down the mountain or anything.

On the other hand, I didn't expect her to say what I overheard in the lodge a little later, either. Addie was sitting with Claire and Dana, sipping her hot cocoa at a table not far from where I was sitting with Sam, Felicia, and Josh. I heard Claire say, "I could have sworn I saw you coming down the trail with Jenny McAfee."

Addie nodded. "Yeah, I guess you could say we took that last run together."

"Why?" Dana asked her.

I sat there, ears peeled, trying to hear how Addie was going to explain what happened on the mountain.

"I don't know," Addie answered her. "I was kind of surprised to see her on a beginner trail after all her bragging about her skiing, and having all those tags on her old jacket. But there she was."

I shrugged. At least Addie wasn't saying anything too mean.

"Anyway, she just insisted on going down the mountain with me," Addie continued. "I think she was tired or something, and kind of afraid of going down herself. So I skied down with her. No big deal."

Grrrr . . . I couldn't believe she had lied like that! *I* was afraid? If it hadn't been for me, Addie would still be sitting there, crying at the top of a beginner slope, the one *she* had been afraid to ski down!

For a minute I felt like jumping up and telling Dana the truth, but I stopped myself. There would be no point in that. She wouldn't believe me, anyway. Especially since Addie would just keep on lying about it.

And then, all of a sudden, I wasn't mad at Addie

anymore. I actually felt sorry for her. She had to lie to her friends all the time in order to make them think she was worth hanging out with. That was actually pretty sad.

I couldn't imagine how awful it would be to have to be fake all the time. I don't have to lie or make things up just to be accepted by my crowd. My friends accept me for who I am. Even if what Addie had said had been true – which it most definitely wasn't – they wouldn't have cared. My friends don't hang around with me because I can ski, or because I have a fashionable new outfit. They hang out with me because they like me. And I hang out with them because I like them. Every one of them. Exactly the way they are. The way I see it, the Pops may be the cool kids, but my friends and I are the lucky ones.

Chapter
TEN

THE SKI TRIP was a distant memory by the following Wednesday afternoon when Sam, Chloe, Liza, and I were hanging out in Liza's kitchen, trying to come up with something to do with our buddies the next day.

"How about making flash cards of sight words?" Liza suggested.

Chloe just shrugged. "I don't know," she said with a lack of enthusiasm. "There's nothing special in that."

"It's educational, though," Liza said. "And maybe we can find some way to make it fun."

"*Fun* flash cards?" Chloe sounded dubious.

"What if we give them treats after they make the flash cards?" I suggested. "That way they can learn sight words, and eat something delicious."

"That's a great idea!" Sam exclaimed.

"What kind of treats?" Liza asked me.

"I don't know," I admitted. "But I bet we can find something great on middleschoolsurvival.com."

And I was right. A moment later, we'd gone onto the site and found something that was perfect. Snowman-shaped cereal treats.

"We have to make eight of them," Chloe said.

"We'd better make extras," I suggested. "Just in case. I bet there'll be a lot of requests for seconds."

"You're right," Liza agreed. "And *we* might want seconds, too." She studied the recipe. "We have all this stuff right here. Let's get started."

As Liza went to get her mom to help us with the oven, I looked over the recipe. It seemed pretty easy.

Cereal Snowmen Treats

Winter's here! It's time to build some snowmen! But you don't need to get all cold and wet to make these snowy treats. You can do it right in your warm, dry kitchen!

YOU WILL NEED:

3 tablespoons butter or margarine

1 tsp. vanilla extract

1 package of mini marshmallows

6 cups crispy rice cereal

wax paper

1 container white frosting

¼ cup mini red hots

½ cup gumdrops

¼ cup chocolate chips

10–20 mini pretzel sticks

an adult to handle the hot stuff

HERE'S WHAT YOU DO:

1. Melt butter or margarine in the microwave in a large bowl.

2. Add vanilla and marshmallows.

3. Pop back in the microwave for 30 second intervals until marshmallow mixture is melted. Stir between each interval.

4. Add the crispy rice cereal.

5. Stir until all the cereal is coated with the butter and marshmallow mixture.

6. Line a large cookie sheet with wax paper. When the marshmallow–cereal mixture is cool enough to touch, rub a little margarine or butter on your hands and form the cereal mixture into balls. Now it's time to build your snowmen! Work quickly while the mixture is still warm.

7. Each snowman will be made from two balls — a larger one and a smaller one. Use about 3/4 cup of the mixture for the bodies and 1/3 cup for the heads. Make five large balls and five smaller ones.

8. Set your larger ball on the wax–paper–lined cookie sheet. Place the small ball on top of the larger ball. You can use a little frosting to hold the two balls together.

9. Now it's decorating time! Use the frosting as glue

when you attach your decorations. Here are some
suggestions: Use the red hots for buttons or for a
nose. A gumdrop makes a tasty hat. Chocolate chips
are great for making eyes or mouths. And pretzel
sticks are perfect for arms.

Makes five snowmen.

When the snowmen were finished, we lined them up on
Liza's kitchen counter. They looked so cheerful and happy.
"Those are absolutely brill!" Sam exclaimed happily.

"Almost too cute to eat," I agreed.

"Almost," Chloe echoed. "But I bet the kids will scarf
them down in seconds."

"They're going to be so happy," Liza agreed.

"No other buddies are going to have anything like
them," Chloe said.

We all stared at her. Once again Chloe had dared to
say what we'd all been thinking, but didn't want to say.
Somehow, this whole buddy program had turned into a
competition with the Pops. And not just the middle
school Pops. Addie and her friends had created a whole
crowd of mini-Pops. Which meant there were mini *non*-
Pops, too.

I knew just how bad our buddies must have been feeling about that. I glanced over at the smiling snowmen on
the kitchen counter. I hoped a couple of tasty treats would
make them feel better.

*   *   *

"Jenny! You're here!" Sofia shouted as I walked into her classroom the next afternoon. She raced over and gave me a big hug.

I smiled and hugged her back. "I wouldn't miss a buddy afternoon," I assured her.

"I know," Sofia answered. "It's just good to see you." She pulled me over to where she, Madison, Shannon, and Carly were sitting. I noticed Taylor, Elizabeth, and Jillian were also grouped together, trying to braid one another's hair. Boy, were their mothers going to have a tough time combing *those* knots out!

"Wait until you guys see what we have for you," Chloe told her buddy, Carly.

"What?" Madison asked.

"It's a surprise," Chloe answered. "And it's just for you, Sofia, Shannon, and Carly."

I frowned slightly. I knew Chloe was trying to make our girls feel special, but I kind of wished she hadn't played into the whole us-and-them thing.

"Can we see the surprise?" Shannon asked.

Liza shook her head. "First we're going to do some reading work. Then, you'll get the surprise."

"Can't we have the surprise first?" Sofia asked.

"There's a reason they call them afters," Sam told her.

"After what?" Madison asked.

I giggled. I'd known Sam long enough now to know that "afters" was a British word for dessert. Sam had just given them a hint, but the girls didn't know it.

"Come on," Liza told the girls cheerfully. "The sooner we make sight-word flash cards, the sooner you can have your surprises."

That was all it took. A moment later our buddies were busy writing words like THE, IN, ON, WE, and ME on their cards. It didn't take them long, and as soon they were finished, they were demanding their surprises.

"Come on, you promised," Sofia reminded me.

"I know," I told her.

"Here you go," Liza said. She reached into the shopping bag she'd brought to class with her and pulled out each of the individually wrapped snowman treats.

"Wow!" Carly squealed.

"Yummy!" Shannon added.

"I'm going to eat his head first," Madison said.

"Not me," Sofia said with an impish grin. "I'm going to take a big bite out of his behind!" The other girls all laughed. (Okay, I admit it. My friends and I giggled at that, too. But it's okay to act childish when you're around little kids, right?)

It was fun to watch the kindergartners eating their snowmen. They seemed so happy, like nothing was bothering them at all. I was glad. After all, that was the whole point.

A few minutes later, Jillian walked over to where we were sitting. "What are you guys doing?" she asked.

"Eating snowmen's rear ends," Sofia said, and our little group broke into a fresh round of giggles.

"Can I have some?" Jillian asked her.

"Aren't you doing something cool and fun with *your* buddies?" Shannon wondered.

Jillian shook her head. "We were making collages of outfits, using pictures from magazines. But it's kind of boring. And our buddies aren't really paying attention to us."

I looked over to where the Pops were sitting. Sure enough, Addie and her friends were busy poring over their fashion magazines. They hadn't even noticed that Jillian wasn't sitting with them anymore.

"We have more snowmen," I told Jillian. "Do you want one?"

Jillian nodded. "Do you have one for Taylor and Elizabeth, too?" she asked shyly.

I nodded. "Why don't you go get them?"

Chloe shot me a look. "What did you do that for?" she asked,

"I feel bad for them," I explained. "They're just little kids."

A moment later, Jillian, Taylor, and Elizabeth were all happily laughing and smiling with Carly, Shannon, Sofia, and Madison. A few of the boys had come over and now they were eating snowmen, too. I was definitely glad we'd made extras. No one would be getting seconds. But that was okay. At least this way nobody who wanted a snowman treat had felt left out.

I grinned as I watched Sofia and Jillian giggling

about eating snowman rear ends. They obviously thought the treats were delicious. But those snowmen had done a lot more than just taste good. They'd managed to unite a whole class of kids! There were no more groups in the kindergarten class. All the girls were friends again!

I thought about my days in kindergarten, back when arguments could be solved easily. I'd been really happy, then. I hardly ever got mad at anyone. And I never worried about what I was wearing, or who my friends were. I was friendly with everyone. Those had been really good times.

Still, as I watched Liza, Sam, and Chloe happily chowing down on their snowman treats, I realized that these were good times, too. *Really* good times. And I wondered if one day I would look back at middle school and only remember the fun I had.

That was possible. Because with friends like mine, surviving middle school was actually a pretty good time!

Red . . . Redder . . . Reddest

Where do you stand on the embarrassment meter? Do you turn red at the slightest thing, or are you able to laugh off even the most horrifyingly embarrassing moments? Take this quiz and see how your behavior measures up.

1. **Uh-oh! You read the Spirit Week schedule wrong. Now you're dressed for pajama day – a day early! How do you handle this fashion disaster?**

   A. Call home for a change of clothes and then hide in the bathroom until your mom arrives with your jeans and T-shirt.
   B. Tell everyone you meant to dress in pjs — just in case you fall asleep in science again.
   C. Change into your gym clothes. Even ugly shorts and a dirty T-shirt are better than slippers and flannel pjs.

2. You have to make a speech in English class. About halfway through your presentation, you lose your train of thought and forget what you wanted to say. What now?

A. Ad lib. You wrote the speech, so no one can tell if you're doing it right or wrong.

B. Stammer, gulp, and quickly say, "That's all I have to say." Then run to your seat.

C. Take a second to regain your thoughts, and continue with your speech the way you meant to.

3. You're on a field trip when you tear your jeans right across the butt. How do you handle this fashion emergency?

A. Make sure you're always in the back of the line, and keep your hands behind you, so no one in your class can see what has happened.

B. Pretend you feel sick so you can go back and sit on the bus for the rest of the trip.

C. Tie your sweatshirt around your waist and go on having fun.

4. You are wearing a new jacket for the first time. The school fashionista passes you in the hall and gives your coat a big thumbs-down. Now what?

A. Immediately shove the jacket in your locker, where it will stay for the rest of the year.

B. Wear your new jacket proudly. You like it, and that's all that matters.

C. Wear it for the rest of the day, then pass it down to your younger cousin. Maybe it will go over better in her school.

5. **The class is taking a science test. The room is completely silent. Then suddenly you let out some gas – loudly! What do you do?**

   A. Begin to cry — this is the worst thing ever!
   B. Laugh first, so everyone will be laughing with you, not at you.
   C. Look around, pretending you weren't the culprit.

6. **Your mom and dad take you to a show where the first act is a hypnotist who is choosing volunteers from the audience. What's your reaction?**

   A. Raise your hand high and volunteer to be the one who will bark like a dog when a bell rings.
   B. You don't volunteer, but if you're called on, you'll go onstage.
   C. You sink down far into your seat, and hide behind the big guy in the chair in front of you.

7. **You've finally gotten the chance to talk to that cute boy from your PE class. It's all going great until he mentions that you have spinach in your teeth. How do you react?**

   A. Cover your mouth with your notebook and continue the conversation.
   B. Excuse yourself and run off to the bathroom for a quick rinse and spit.
   C. Laugh, and say, "Great! I'm still kind of hungry, anyway."

8. **You're walking around in the mall when you spot someone who is wearing your friend's coat and has the same haircut. You call out her name over and over again. Unfortunately, when the girl turns around, you realize it's not her. It's a complete stranger. What do you do?**

A. Quickly dive into the nearest store and hope the stranger didn't see you.

B. Smile, explain that you thought she was someone else, and introduce yourself.

C. Apologize for the confusion and scurry away as fast as your feet will take you.

It's time to see just how embarrassed you can get. First tally up your score. Then check the chart to see how you react to embarrassing situations.

1. A. 1 point   B. 3 points   C. 2 points
2. A. 3 points   B. 1 point   C. 2 points
3. A. 2 points   B. 1 point   C. 3 points
4. A. 1 point   B. 3 points   C. 2 points
5. A. 1 point   B. 3 points   C. 2 points
6. A. 3 points   B. 2 points   C. 1 point
7. A. 2 points   B. 1 point   C. 3 points
8. A. 1 point   B. 3 points   C. 2 points

8-12 points: You definitely embarrass easily. But look at the bright side. You'll never have to spend money on blush. Your cheeks are red enough on their own. Seriously though, try to learn to accept that silly mistakes happen to everyone from time to time.

13-18 points: Like most people, you do get embarrassed from time to time. But for the most part you take your mishaps in stride. Good for you!

19-24 points: Three cheers for you — and the louder the better. That way everyone will turn and stare at you. Which is exactly the way you like it! Congrats for having a sense of humor that allows you to laugh at yourself, no matter what life brings.

Take a sneak peek at the next book in the

HOW I SURVIVED MIDDLE SCHOOL

series:

Caught in the Web